THE
OCEAN
HOUSE

Also by Mary-Beth Hughes

The Loved Ones

Double Happiness

Wavemaker II

THE OCEAN HOUSE

Stories

MARY-BETH HUGHES

Atlantic Monthly Press
New York

FIRST EDITION

Published simultaneously in Canada
Printed in Canada

First Grove Atlantic hardcover edition: January 2021

This book is set in 1.5-pt. Scala LF
by Alpha Design and Composition of Pittsfield, NH.

Library of Congress Cataloging-in-Publication data
available for this title.

ISBN 978-0-8021-5753-9
eISBN 978-0-8021-5754-6

Atlantic Monthly Press
an imprint of Grove Atlantic
154 West 14th Street
New York, NY 10011

Distributed by Publishers Group West

groveatlantic.com

21 22 23 24   10 9 8 7 6 5 4 3 2 1

For Duke,
and for Pod,
all my love.

THE
OCEAN
HOUSE

CONTENTS

THE OCEAN HOUSE

They were tiny girls lying on their bellies by the wide windows of the playroom, spying on their mother far below. She tiptoed along the seawall, holding steady on puddled dips and sharp edges of the black jetty. Waves burst and sprayed at her feet. The girls pressed in close, touching clouds and crabs etched in the glass along the lower rims. Their fingers worked into the grooves as they watched their mother—so light-footed, her bathing suit beneath a sundress—climb over the fence between the neighboring beach club property and their own. She's a fish! their father liked to declare, but she didn't like to be *inside* the ocean. She preferred salt water in a swimming pool where she could see the beginning and end.

Midmorning, Mrs. Hoving, despite her bad hip, walked all the way down the back stairs to retrieve milk and peaches. Their playroom was a round attic room on the turret end. But directly below, the grandest room of the house was empty. In the master bedroom a plinth raised the bed so high that, waking, their mother might see the waves first thing. Above the bed, a built-in carved canopy of shells and rosebuds lifted by four columns all painted white. The vista windows had ribbons of more rosebuds in pale-pink stained glass; the thorns were blunt and blue. A sleeping place for a sea queen. But their mother didn't care for it. Thought it corny, trite. The window shade manufacturer's silly dream for a wife who left him anyway. Then he went bankrupt. Why would she want to sleep there?

Their mother was content in a regular rectangular bedroom with cross breezes. Besides, the grand circular bedroom with the plinth, the canopy, the flat pink glass roses and stubby thorns was haunted by a small boy who swung by his feet and made slurping noises nibbling at the sleeper's nose. Their mother said he liked to be left alone.

Of course they wanted to know how old he was, but she couldn't say, which was frustrating because age was crucial to them at the time. Courtney was five, nearly five. Paige was three. Their mother was twenty-seven, so an old woman she said. Their father twenty-eight. But they were a year and a half apart, like Courtney and Paige. Mrs. Hoving claimed to be 103.

On the turret side of the house, below the haunted bedroom, was the circular dining room. Lower still, a cellar of sand and rock, entirely off-limits. But in the bright round dining room, where they were free to come and go, their mother hung a new wallpaper. She'd imported the white herons standing in the lime-colored reeds from Japan. The house made me do it, she said. And that made sense because it looked, when she was finished, as if it had been here from the start. Something to appease the fleeing wife, the broken husband, the hungry boy. All of them.

Don't be flip, said their father, as if she'd said something cruel. Mrs. Hoving didn't allow cruelty. Nor did their mother. Their father could be changeable on this point.

The year was 1962. The house except for the newly arrived Japanese herons—and their bending inquiring white necks—was ninety years old at the time but seemed much older. It was the last of the great oceanfront houses left in Long Branch.

Built in the same exuberant era, the Beach Club aimed for grandeur, too, with its herringbone boardwalk and a vast saltwater pool, the cunning trellised card room, the vaulted seaside dining terrace, the clubhouse itself, like a vast white Victorian wedding cake. A cliché, said their mother. It was meant to seduce those living in the houses who had plenty to keep them at home. But later, with the towers, business improved.

The Beach Club stood directly north of their house. Its property continued for about an eighth of a mile until it petered out—their mother shrugged—at the tennis courts, then the high jagged jetty wall picked up again and continued along the Ocean Avenue for a while before crossing the town line into Sea Bright, which was filled with newer beach clubs vying for sunbathers and swimmers. To the south toward Asbury Park, all the new slinky apartment towers lined up, with concrete balconies like gray tongues that stuck out on the ocean side only. Tucked in, here and there, were the few other survivors. A nunnery. Two oil tycoons in retirement. Syrian Jews. And next to them, the Lebanese Catholics. Houses like their own, shingled and sometimes sagging, behind iron gates and high hedges.

The Beach Club was eager to tear down their house and build its own tower. Sheep, said their mother. Sheep with demolition kits.

When the house first came up for sale—something quick and private to settle a complicated estate—the club lost the bid. And their father won *because*, their mother said, of his exceptionally good character. And also the windfall that came to their mother quite by surprise, a gift sent from overseas. Money that had once been her own mother's now all these years later released to her. They paid cash, she told the girls, and Courtney liked to think of a wheelbarrow full of bills and coins.

The club president never gave up about the house. He's a terrier! said their mother. A sheep, a terrier, a snake, the shape and sound of his threat changed day to day. Baa, woof, hiss.

At least he can't sue, said their father. He can only send spiteful letters.

But he can, true? He may do much worse.

This over breakfast coffee in the human-scale kitchen, another rectangle, whitewashed beadboard to the chair rail, then blue plaster walls. And bluish morning light off the ocean through the windows to match. Mrs. Hoving scraping carrots into shreds at the sink. For later. Their father would welcome a lawsuit. That would settle things for good. Though of course there are no grounds, he said.

But there were. And this was something Courtney would look into much later, the shady deal that briefly gave them their beautiful house and then allowed them to lose it. And she would think about the wheelbarrow full of money.

Still, at the time, the girls understood a truce had been struck with the Beach Club about their mother's essential swimming. She was allowed in the pool. Soon, she would bring them, too. When they were ready to learn to swim. The girls believed all of this was an extraordinary concession. For their mother, who deserved special treatment. But it turned out they'd had a membership all the years they lived next door. Something that evaporated when they left and moved inland away from the ocean. As if without their mother they were no longer welcome at the Beach Club. So the special-treatment theory held steady for a long time.

In those years, they'd never use the club's front entrance. Like their mother, they'd learn to pick their way over the slick jetty, a shortcut. By their own front gate, a too-grand affair of iron curlicues, black-green cypress spires grew high enough to block out the sight of the summer traffic and to screen their mother's chosen bedroom from any prying eyes.

She especially liked the room for its red marble mantle, which reminded her of London. In summertime, the windows would be thrown open and the hum of car engines on the avenue and the bang and hiss of the waves would rush in all together. The lion-skin carpet at the foot of her bed had a doggy smell.

The only pet you'll ever have, my loves, said their mother, who was against keeping animals because of what had happened to her dog in the war.

As they grew older, their mother spoke more about her life in London. One morning in London, for instance, their grandmother Bess—whom they'd never meet, though Paige had her dark round eyes exactly—one morning their grandmother put their mother, seven years old, on a train to the country. With other girls just like you their mother told them. She had a fat ham sandwich and a clean blue dress folded in a paper sack. Ten weeks later she came home to a crater in the sidewalk. And all because their grandmother Bess refused to fold up her food tent just for the sound of yet another sputtering engine in the sky. Beneath a white fluttery tablecloth strung up on poles to keep out the sun overhead, Bess gave sandwiches to anyone in need. Her card table set at the end of the front walk. Samson the beagle lay at her feet, ready to ward off danger if it came along. From above, among gray stone houses and gray roads and rooftops the white tablecloth must have shone clear.

But when they were still tiny enough to keep to the playroom, the most frightening thing they believed their mother knew was the hungry boy who swung upside down over the deserted master bed. She was keeping clear of him.

Far below, their mother on the tips of her toes stepped off the seawall, her sundress fluttering away from her in the wind, her famous black swimsuit just visible when she straddled the Beach Club fence. Mrs. Hoving's cool hands fell on their shoulders smelling of peaches. Come away from the window now, girls. Let your mother have a bit of peace.

Later their father moved them two miles inland. The new house in the neighborhood behind Our Lady Star of the Sea had a flat lawn, closets with louvered doors on metal tracks, and a screened-in porch where their new stepmother, Ruth, would set up shop, she said, until it was time to switch the thermostat up in the fall. Then her friends would visit in the den. If the girls needed permission for anything, they always knew where to find her. She had a voice that carried and wanted them to talk louder, too. And stop walking so much on their tiptoes. They were quiet girls, especially Paige. The elder, Courtney, ten turning eleven when they moved to Honeysuckle Lane, often spoke for them both now.

Once they were settled in, their father decided he'd keep the ocean house a while longer.

What for? asked Ruth, taken aback. You won't see a better offer. This is it, the sky-high limit. Trust me.

Their father winked at the girls. Oh, I might hear something a *little* more persuasive. And they smiled. This was the old game they knew.

Okay, said Ruth. Not my beeswax.

From Honeysuckle Lane the girls could walk themselves to school. Ten minutes flat, back door to Star of the Sea parking lot. A new school for the girls, they were Catholics now, like Ruth. Their mother had been agnostic. Just in case, she'd said. Their mother let them wear shoes whenever they liked. Ruth handed out their school shoes only in the mudroom. She didn't want them tracking in the muck of their shortcut through Mr. Kemp's apple orchard. The whole house would stink of rot, like stale cider then.

Mr. Kemp's shortcut was mostly avoided by the neighborhood kids. The old orchard was overgrown and dense with pricker bushes and poison sumac. Paige spotted three snakes and a water rat on a single afternoon. Once they saw a group of boys from the seventh and eighth grade smoking cigarettes and sitting on a fallen tree trunk by a half-collapsed wood structure, an old outhouse. A thorny holly sealed up the door. It was a windbreak, and the boys squeezed the still-lit butts though the cut sliver moon in the door, as if daring the place to catch fire. Courtney and Paige walked the farthest path then, heads down to avoid notice.

But one day Courtney had detention after school. While Sister Joseph was sorting the attendance book entries, a counting mistake she couldn't make sense of, Courtney let out a fake sneeze that had words embedded inside: Aren't you? Aren't you fat?

Silence, Sister Joseph said. Heads up.

And Courtney whispered something about the knot in Sister's forehead, a mysterious lump that popped out between her eyebrows.

Don't move! shouted Sister. Freeze! Then, when she'd fully assessed the class: Courtney Ruddy? Right here, right now.

Sister pointed to a spot near the chalked detention list. Add your name and stay right there.

And Courtney felt her face go hot red with the effort to keep it still, not to laugh or cry. Made to stand against the blackboard until dismissal and not wriggle, then given the task of stacking the chairs in the corridor, all thirty of them.

On the way home, her boots unzipped, her coat unbuttoned, seeking penance, Courtney heard her sister Paige's voice. A shiver of a laugh for the kind of ugly joke they might tell each other in the night, a supposition about Ruth and her wide fanny. Or the big bosom they liked to wrap their arms around, Paige in front, Courtney behind, then re-create the shape of, amazed. It was that same laugh, a bit of a hiss, but she couldn't see Paige. The trees in October were already scratchy tangles against a gray sky, so there was no place to hide except the outhouse. And there she was, standing with her back to the outhouse door, a big boy—maybe a seventh grader, maybe even an eighth grader—pressed against her. His arms stretched high, fingers splayed on the wood. Paige's head stuck out just beneath his armpit. He angled his big body like a plank into Paige. Don't, she said, without a laugh now.

One big boy said, He's only playing. But Paige said, I can feel his thing!

Courtney kept walking to her sister. She didn't speed up and she didn't slow down. She closed her coat carefully as if the motion might break something. When she was near enough to be heard, she said, Hey?

They all looked at her at once.

Are you all right? she said directly to her sister. Courtney made her eyes simple. Pretending she was just a wispy leaf, maybe orange colored, that had landed on Paige, nothing to be scared of.

The boys looked at Courtney. There were more than she'd thought; some had cigarettes burning.

Are you okay? Courtney tried again.

No one answered her. And when Paige looked at her, her eyes went blank, as if she were a door Courtney couldn't go through today.

Courtney didn't want to say her sister's name, in case the boys didn't know it, so they wouldn't be able to find her later or the house on Honeysuckle Lane. Should I wait? she said to Paige.

Nope, said a boy with black hair and pink cheeks. Everything's fine. We're playing a game.

Paige, under the boy's armpit, looked so small. At least her coat was buttoned. Go home, Courtney. It's a game, she said, but Paige sounded like the doll talking when the string was pulled: Go home.

Courtney turned around and started walking, feeling the way she had earlier today when everyone looked at her as they left the classroom. Sister Joseph had succeeded in marking her as repulsive as her own wart. And now the big boys could see this about Courtney, too. It was as clear to them as Sister Joseph's protuberance. Ruth's word, giving the big lump with gray hair sprouting out like a spare eyebrow some dignity. Courtney was a protuberance. The boys liked her sister and wanted nothing to do with Courtney.

But then maybe Paige was only faking. She was often a liar now. They both were. Courtney spun back whether they wanted her to or not, but they'd taken their game elsewhere. Quiet as snakes, they'd already vanished from the orchard.

When Courtney got home, Ruth was serving sweet pickled onions on pumpernickel toast rounds in the den for four o'clock cocktails. She waved Courtney upstairs, sighing: Homework, please.

Don't you care where precious Paige is? whispered Courtney.

But Ruth was repeating her sigh, more amplified now for her friends. Upstairs in the room she shared with Paige, the lavender flounce on Courtney's twin canopy bed looked stupid. She ripped the ruffles off hoping to get rid of it once and for all. But she left the top of Paige's bed intact so she could make her own decision.

* * *

In the ocean house their mother had been against ruffles.
Forced down your throats your entire lives, why start now.
They were dressed like little English girls in gray and navy
blue, good linens, good wools. They wore their hair in single
braids, tied beginning and end with white cotton ribbon. Mrs.
Hoving did the brushing and the braiding and the baths with
the transparent brown soap.

Mrs. Hoving vanished when they moved to Honeysuckle
Lane. They asked their father where she'd gone. And Ruth
answered quickly: To Newark, to her family. Lots of trouble
there and she's the only one with any sense.

Would Mrs. Hoving be coming back when the trouble
was over?

Now why would she, asked Ruth. And the girls looked
to their father for confirmation, but he was busy watching
out the window, guarding the flat lawn.

After the day in the orchard with the boys at the old outhouse,
Paige told Courtney she wasn't allowed there anymore. The
boys have made it out-of-bounds.

For both of us?

No, Paige said. Just for you. And just in the afternoon.
The morning it's still fine to cut through.

Which meant Courtney now had to take the long
route home all the way down Oakes Road to the far end of

12

Honeysuckle Lane. She was the only one walking this way. But soon Andrew Kennedy cycled slowly around her, an eighth grader with big flat hands and coat hanger shoulders, stiff and pointing. A shorter, thinner older brother's school blazer riding up to reveal the pale skin above his flannel trousers. This bike's only four years old, he explained. It's still perfect. As if Courtney wanted to know. He tipped sideways to tighten the loops around her, stinking the air with pockets of his breath and sweat. He made her dizzy, just to look at him. You don't frighten me, she said. They were out in the wide open and any neighbor or even Ruth might drive by in an instant. But every day now included a blister of time with Andrew Kennedy and his chipped green three speed.

What does he want? asked Paige, from the top of her pristine bed. She always made it up carefully and slipped into the sheets and blankets at the last minute just to sleep.

He must be lonely, said Courtney, though it had never occurred to her before. Those boys still in the orchard?

Not really, said Paige. Then she was pulling back the bedspread as if it stank of something and inserting her skinny legs one at a time into Ruth's stiff bleached sheets.

Courtney was the oldest in the fifth grade at Star of the Sea. She'd been left back the year they moved to Honeysuckle Lane. Now Paige in fourth had almost caught up to her. Courtney had started out smart but now she was in the bottom percentile.

She's not much of a trier, Ruth explained to their father. Ruth had done her best. But given the steep task and the short time allotted, there was talk of cutting losses. Sometimes the older takes the brunt, she said. We have to face facts.

And Courtney, folded into her hiding spot between the back of the tweed sofa and the heating vent, assumed she'd be sent away like Mrs. Hoving, so the more promising Paige could be given more of what Ruth had to offer.

Paige is a sweet thing, so helpful. But it was the dead of winter, their father pointed out, as if that were relevant. As if when the snow lifted, Courtney might bloom again. This point was met with silence.

When the spring finally came, the orchard filled in with blossoms and then the buds of tiny apples-to-be. The fruit already at Mr. Kemp's farm stand was imported. Ruth shopped there and one evening told their father that Mr. Kemp had made a pass at her, had tried to rub his nasty fingers where they don't belong.

The girls didn't believe it.

Handed me my bag of cherries and nearly twisted a you know what off me. Their father laughed, and Ruth laughed, too.

Oh, such a rookie, he said.

At afternoon cocktails, Ruth often related the woes of her new life. The girls were stubborn, selfish, contrary, though never rude. I'll give their mother that much, she'd say. She taught them manners. Too much, if you ask me.

Never rude? Of course not! Their mother was born in England, her own mother, Bess, gone early in the war. Her father earlier still.

Sometimes Ruth pumped them for information so urgently the girls wondered if their father ever told her anything at all.

They do the snaky dance and that's it, said Paige. Courtney caught their father in the kitchen rubbing his front against Ruth's bottom. When Courtney arrived with dessert plates he wheeled back and pretended a golf swing. He doesn't even play golf, said Courtney later to Paige.

One thing Ruth really wanted to know was who found their mother first. She didn't lead up to it, just asked outright. So? Ruth pressed. The girls looked astonished. Or at least that's how Ruth described them to the afternoon ladies. Mouths hanging open, eyes like marbles, she said. She had her work cut out for her with those two, all right.

Sometimes a shock like that does brain damage, she said.

The women agreed, but also said they liked her new egg salad. Catsup, Ruth confided. It's my secret.

When Ruth whimpered late in the night on the other side of the wall and woke up the girls, they decided that their father was shaking catsup on her bottom. This was the funniest thing in the world but also nauseating. Paige would go into the yellow bathroom and put her finger down her throat until nothing came up but green. She'd come back into bed, stinking of stomach juice.

Are the boys nice to you? asked Courtney.

What boys? said Paige.

Let me show you something, said Courtney. She got up and gathered her seashells off the top of her dresser. Sometimes, if I put these in a special order—she arranged a circle of shells with two brownish sand-encrusted fragments in the center—Mama just appears.

Shut up, said Paige.

Not in the firm way, more in a dreamy way.

On your canopy, I suppose. Just shut up.

That was only a story, said Courtney. That was pretend. Then she swept up her shells and put them in a drawer where they wouldn't get contaminated.

It wasn't Paige, as they'd sworn to Ruth, but Courtney who first found their mother. And right away, Courtney knew she was the lucky one. Worse to have to make up a picture in your mind to fill such a giant meaning. The actual picture was of their mother asleep on the lion rug. Curled almost like a kitten, one leg stretched out, the other tucked in. She lay on her side, and the cheek not covered by her hair rested close to but not exactly on the lion's paw. Her cheek was mottled and only slightly gray. Courtney came in to tell her that nothing Mrs. Hoving said on the ride home from school made sense yet and it had been a whole week of speaking French in the car and it still didn't mean anything beyond *bonjour* and *je t'aime*. Her mother's sundress was lifted all the way to her waist as if to cool her legs off. Bonjour, Maman. Je t'aime. Her favorite bathing suit, the black one, was loose around the tops of her thighs. Je t'aime, Maman. Her mother was being too careful lately with her diet.

Thirty-three years old is awfully young to have a tricky heart, said one of the women in the den. My goodness.

It wasn't quite so simple, said Ruth and then whispered her motto about small ears and big mouths. They could all see Courtney at the kitchen counter.

Looking for the oranges, dear? called out Ruth like she was the darling wife and mother in a black-and-white movie. So many people liked her for what she was doing. The neighborhood women who sat with her, drinking gin and tonics, admired her and said so. You're a trooper, Ruth.

They'd never seen her in the days when she wasn't a trooper at all. Ruth at the Beach Club snack bar, dipping the French fry basket into bubbling oil. Then she was Mrs. Carter, and one day she had a chevron-shape burn like a red arrow stuck on her forearm. Hard not to get hurt in such tight quarters.

She's blind and foolish just like me, their mother said. It was a hot day and her temper got the better of her. That's how she explained it. Later when they were back over the fence, back on their own rocks, tiptoeing toward the back steps. The heebie-jeebies, the creeps.

It's not that poor woman's fault, their mother said.

The first summer on Honeysuckle Lane and the first without the Beach Club. In fact no ocean at all, which was strange. They were still quite close. But Ruth preferred a day camp for the girls, with itchy woodland hikes and swim practice in a scummy chlorine pool.

They were both older now than their mother had been on the day she returned to London from the safe countryside to find only the crater where her house had been. And when Ruth was being annoying, going through their dresser drawers, insisting on a particular order to their underwear, Paige would whisper to Courtney: At least she's not as bad as the crater. Which was funny but not very.

When she was returned by train to London, with the other children, their mother was able to find an aunt to help her—really only a courtesy aunt, a neighbor named Florence Kinney. And their father liked to say how resourceful their mother was and, for a little girl, how very brave.

In the ocean house, down the hall from her bedroom, their mother made a kind of dressing room of a windowless storage closet. There, inside a cigar box, she kept the striped handkerchief she wore around her neck in case she needed it as a mask at the end of the war. In Hampstead the air was often filled with ash. And every single day, Florence Kinney would say it was all beyond her. The care of a child in this misery was completely outside her ken. Every other person had a crater, after all, but not everyone had an orphan thrust her way.

That's why when their mother was very tired or had the heebie-jeebies or the creeps, their own father knelt beside her and put his arms around her legs, as if she were only a tiny girl, like them. In the house by the ocean everyone who needed a mother had one. This was their joke as a family. A surplus of mothers. Mrs. Hoving thought this was funny, too, because of course she was one of them. Their father held their mother tight around her knees until she laughed, saying: Off! you're a nuisance, her fingers curled soft around his wrists.

In mid-August, everyone on Honeysuckle Lane was asked by the Long Branch township to stay home and indoors as much as possible while the authorities cleaned up the mess and the danger after the surprise hurricane. This came over the radio.

Though the rain itself lasted less than a day and a night, the rivers and creeks overflowed, taking bits and pieces from the waterfront inland. A dinghy landed as far as the lawn at the end of Honeysuckle Lane. And the Beach Club and all the towers went dark.

As soon as Ocean Avenue was passable, defying municipal orders, Ruth loaded the girls in the car for some fresh air and a little snooping. She'd had some news, she said. Through the grapevine. They'd go investigate if it was true.

The ocean house belonged to their father, of course—completely, irrevocably. But now the town—in a plot!—was considering some kind of eminent domain. All because the seawall had been breached for half an hour!

They were going to see this travesty in motion. The girls didn't know what Ruth was talking about. But now they waited on the sodden salt-burned grass behind the cypress trees while Ruth spoke to a police officer who'd set up a table in their old seashell driveway. Firemen in high waders came by and drank water from Dixie cups then pulled masks down over their faces and went up the high white-painted back steps where the girls once liked to hang their bathing suits on the railing to dry.

Inside, said the policeman—a grouchy man with a wide flat nose—the water had made a mark, like a finger run all along the dining room wall. A grubby, little girl's finger, he said to Paige. Someone who didn't wash her hands before dinner.

That's enough of you, said Ruth. But too late, they could see the slimy trail marking their mother's Japanese silk wallpaper. Through the white herons and the reeds. About three feet high, said the policeman to Ruth. I swear it.

All a charade, said Ruth. I don't believe a word. A finger mark on a dodgy wallpaper? And you're taking a house? Every one of us will be out on our keesters at this rate.

A fireman slogged toward them. He lifted a Dixie cup in a soot-black hand. The house is deserted, he said and smiled down at Ruth in an ugly way. A way that Courtney recognized as pleasure. And felt a funny twitch of being glad for him. Glad for his happiness.

Nothing like it, said Ruth. Not for a minute.

The girls were marched back to the car, and Ruth made the sign—a zip on the lips—of not saying a thing about this adventure to their father.

Despite their silence, at dinner that night their father looked downcast. So he knew. Though he said it was just the weather. That and something about taxes and a faulty plan. A thieving accountant. No recourse. He was speaking in code, to Ruth only, but they could tell by her face the news was shocking and bad. There was a very long pause after he finished talking. Chewing was impossible. Courtney remembers this night after the hurricane, the feeling as if her jaw had been welded shut by all the electrons Ruth said were flooding the air.

Wait, Paige said, as if she'd figured the whole thing out. Maybe things would be much easier if Ruth could just have her wish.

And what's that? asked their father.

They—she and Courtney—could be taken by someone else along with the ocean house for good. Save a lot of trouble all round, Paige said with the slightest fake British accent.

Their father studied Paige: her long straight brown hair, the feathery arch of her eyebrows, her mother's mobile, easily happy mouth, grim now, serious. He studied Paige for a long time, as if in reappraisal, before he answered in the

21

low quiet voice. The voice that told them they didn't need to believe him at all. He said that someday they'd recognize the jewel they had in Ruth.

Right after the hurricane, Mrs. Hoving came to visit Ruth on the screen porch. The back lawn was covered in broken branches of still-green maple leaves. All the jetsam and debris half-swept into piles for the municipal trucks to remove one yard at a time.

Mrs. Hoving had been helping Mrs. Lanahan down the road. She still did a bit of piecework stitching on the side, drapes and so on. She could do light upholstery, too. If Ruth ever needed such help. And she was so nearby today she thought, Oh, let me just lay eyes on the little ones again. Her niece's husband was delayed picking her up, and she said to herself and then to Ruth: I told myself to walk down the lane to where that kind man has made a new home. A new start. But was it true?

Mrs. Lanahan had been full of news about the ocean house. Mrs. Hoving couldn't believe her ears. Condemned?

Courtney came home from school but not Paige. All Mrs. Hoving had time to do in front of Ruth's frowning, scouring eyes was pat Courtney's wrist and say, You always had your mother's pretty hands. Then her niece's husband pulled all the way into the circle drive in a loud Oldsmobile with a discolored bumper. Mrs. Hoving went right out the front door. Just like that, Queen of Sheba, said Ruth to their father that night and imitated a wide sashay that looked nothing like Mrs. Hoving's aching hip or her careful steps.

Did Mrs. Hoving leave a message for me? asked Paige.

She talked about Mama's hands, said Courtney. Probably that was for you, too.

The main thing she said was that she was grateful, said Ruth, yes, very thankful that you two were so well loved now. At long last.

That sounds like a fib, said Paige.

Apologize, said their father.

Paige scraped out her chair and darted out of the dining room and up the staircase. Upstairs, the door to their room slammed shut.

Courtney kept her face averted from Ruth and waited for her father to make sense of the situation. He seemed confused. As if Mrs. Hoving had moved something important or stolen something and left the door wide open to worse. Finally he said, Eat your dinner, now, Courtney. It will only get cold.

It's too gross, she said quietly. But he was distracted, listening, as if he could still discern Paige through the ceiling. I want to puke? whispered Courtney, as if telling her father what he really was listening for. Though he didn't know it yet. Spoiling a surprise.

Oh, for the love of god, said Ruth. That's it! That's it. And she, too, scraped back her chair and let the tears in her eyes show before rushing out, hugging her belly, looking to Courtney like a troll who'd swallowed a poisoned frog.

23

Everyone's so upset, said Courtney with a smile to her father.

Maybe Mrs. Hoving should mind her own business, he said and went off to comfort Ruth.

The night before, Ruth told them that the hurricane had flooded the Olympic-size pool at the Beach Club, so much that waves formed and pushed the French fry cooker out of the boardwalk snack shack and onto the jetty. Only the benches on the boardwalk bolted in place had any chance of staying still, she said, but then the boards buckled up like a wave themselves and the benches went with them. Those that were commemorated—for Mrs. Lawrence Thees and for Miss Ethel Bolmeyer—were retrieved and being repaired first. Their mother didn't have a bench. Which seemed right, since she had a whole house to be remembered by. But the pool rising up was a frightening idea. What if the waves had come high when their mother taught them to swim? She'd hold them tight and leap into the pool and help them flutter up to the surface and find their breath. The two of them so tiny and so strong their mother swam them around and around in her arms until they learned to kick free.

Hurricane or not, the new school year began just after Labor Day. Courtney was in sixth grade now, Paige in the fifth. To get to Star of the Sea they had to climb over and around the storm debris, downed tree limbs still uncollected, some shellacked in a dried greenish sludge. Seaweed.

Red tide, warned Ruth. Don't touch anything.

Now, each morning before she left for school, Courtney arranged her seashells in a straight line, one touching the next, on top of her white dresser. Before she went to sleep at night, she shaped them in the circle. Bon matin, Maman. Bonne nuit. Je t'aime.

The first Friday back at school, she came home and the shells were gone and she knew exactly what had happened. Just to make sure, she stood in the archway to the den. Cocktails and hors d'oeuvres on a tray, Ruth in the middle of a story about Mrs. Hoving. Ruth paused and waited.

I'm cleaning my room, Courtney said.

Ruth sputtered a laugh. Oh, right. But one of the others, a more experienced mother, said, How nice!

But I can't find my seashells. For dusting.

The two women sitting on the tweed sofa smiled. And Ruth caught her cue. Try the bookshelf over your desk? I'll bet that's where they are.

Thank you, said Courtney and went out through the garage to find Paige in the orchard. Paige had told Courtney she was strictly forbidden in the orchard, even in the mornings. No one wanted her in the orchard now. But Paige had taken her best things to give away. Just like she'd taken their father's canon-style cigarette lighter and his English beer.

In the orchard, Paige stood against the outhouse, arms crossed and angry, as Courtney walked toward her along the path. Two boys, Eddie, with the bluish swollen girl's mouth, and Henry, with the pink cheeks, sat on the ground smoking small black cigars. They looked up at Courtney, frowning. The third boy was Andrew Kennedy, leaning back against his tipped-over bike wheel, legs splayed. He didn't look at her at all.

Out, said Paige. Now.

We are out, said Courtney jutting her chin. She stared at her sister's tiny breasts on display, her uniform jumper on the ground. Her Carter's underpants looked stretched out and baggy as if she'd carried things in them. The lighter, the shells. She still wore her school blouse, opened up, but the collar was smudged as if Henry's black cigar and Eddie's blue lips had leaked together there. Her tiny breasts, unlike Courtney's, poked straight out like thumb tips. And the nipples were light small orangey caps on each. Courtney's new breasts were rounder. Ruth junior, Paige had said in a fight, and Courtney worried this might be true. Her nipples looked like stupid pink toy pig pennies. Go away, said Paige. Last warning.

Ruth wants you, Courtney said.

What for?

How should I know? She told me to find you. She said even if you had to stay for detention, tell Sister to let you come home.

Henry stubbed out the black cigar. He stood and popped it through the half-moon slit in the door behind Paige's head. As if she'd disappeared. He didn't need to acknowledge her anymore. She'd failed at something, Courtney knew, and felt a tickle of panic for her sister. Henry's pants were unzipped, but now he fastened them, slid his belt through the loops in slow motion. Buckle, jacket pulled on, his clip-on school tie shoved down into a side pocket. Yeah, he said to the boys. Eddie jerked up his book bag. Andrew Kennedy righted his bike. The three of them zigzagged away through the wrecked trees.

Nice work, Courtney. Paige pulled her uniform jumper on over her head.

Zipper, said Courtney.

Paige smoothed her flyaway hair. They'll tell everyone, you know.

I'll take my shells back now, said Courtney.

Tough luck, detective, said Paige. Too late.

The next week, the second week of sixth grade, Courtney's new teacher, Sister Frances, said they were old enough to know the ins and outs of hell. They weren't babies anymore. They had power. They could pray for those already in hell and for those who were well on the way, stumbling blindly along the dark path.

Paige. Obviously. She'd let boys rummage around in her underpants.

Sister Frances then prompted the prayer for those who had sinned against us. This was the merciful part, the intervention for our enemies. This was all fascinating and not something their mother had agreed with, ever. She had suspended her belief when she was little, she told them, like a balloon. Like a zeppelin! And she seemed to think this was very funny. So Courtney hovered now between whether to try this prayerful intervention for her sister or not. But then she did. She imagined lifting Paige out of her quick certain slide into hell at the last minute, throwing a damp towel over Paige's scorched wispy leaf-tangled hair. She prayed and nothing changed. So on Thursday afternoon Courtney tried her mother again. She hid her mother's play earring, a pearly cluster on a rusty clip, under the bed skirt. She had a candle stub from the kitchen drawer. She nestled the stub in the shag carpet and lit it. The instant the bed skirt caught fire Ruth was banging on the door.

Something about the look of Paige, her legs wide, knee socks high, oxfords laced, backbone lined up at the sagging corner of the old outhouse, hair a nest with dead leaves tangled at the top of her head, underpants hanging in heavy folds, her nipples, her nylon school blouse reminded Courtney of a painting her mother had kept hanging on the wall of her dressing room. Nymphs, water nymphs, bored and dozy-eyed like Paige with bodies that looked electric under the winding fabric mostly on their hips. The nymphs dragged toes through shallow ponds. They sat on rocks or propped their bodies against tree trunks like Paige at the outhouse. Courtney could kill Paige. Just kill her. Paige's underpants all baggy around her legs just like their mother's bathing suit because their mother had become too thin.

Even though their father had tried to fatten her up with barbecued steaks on the grill, salt in the air, blood rolling on

28

their plates. Their mother would lick and chew. Hurry now, said Mrs. Hoving standing at the back door. Come girls. The light still pink over the ocean, Mrs. Hoving tucked them into bed. Then their parents would come and find the exact place on each forehead to efficiently deliver their love. Their father had forgotten all about that. No one was delivering anything anymore. But Paige in the orchard with her baggy pants was transmitting something to the boys on the ground and they were the ones with precision now. Courtney hated her sister for deserting her this way. She truly hated her. And that made her feel very sick in her stomach.

Downstairs in the kitchen, waiting for her father to come home and adjudicate the bed fire, her mother's pearly play earring sitting on a dish like poison, Courtney slumped and still—not a word now, hissed Ruth, not a sound—two things occurred to Courtney. The first thing was that Ruth had knocked before charging in, which she seldom did, and the second was that she must have been right outside the door the whole time, waiting for Courtney to do something bad.

Ruth stood now whisking rye bread crumbs into gravy at the stove top. Potatoes roasting in the oven. A soft, soothing *pop-pop* of gunfire from the den, where Paige, home from school, watched television. When their father came in at dinnertime, Ruth would then wash her hands of Courtney and her obstinate refusal to accept the love and nurturance so abundantly provided. She was finished being treated like the servant, she said, stirring the gravy, rehearsing. This was it.

But their father was in no mood for Courtney. Right away he tried to shoo her into the den with Paige. You stay where you are! said Ruth.

Listen, he needed to talk to Ruth, now, because he wasn't going to let the bastards win.

Of course he wasn't, said Ruth, but she squinted when he put his briefcase down on the chair beside Courtney. He might let the bastards win, her look said. He just might.

And it occurred to Courtney that Ruth washing her hands of all of them might be the answer her mother was giving to the prayer. Her mother would never do anything to hurt Paige, Courtney now understood, even if she did have to go to hell. Their mother had protected Paige against the boy ghost and the ocean. Like their mother, they only swam in the pool. And one time she'd found Paige in the dark rock cellar: I see you, darling. Come out now. She'd been missing for so long, their father had given up and feared the worst. Courtney had forgotten about all that.

Don't move, Ruth said. Don't move a muscle.

But to her father, Courtney had become invisible. The corrupt thieving assholes on the town council, the bastards at the Beach Club. He turned blood red. Courtney knew how this might unfold. Sometimes their mother had hidden them in the ocean house, hidden herself. But Ruth was too stupid and the house too small for really hiding. Courtney slithered down lower in her chair as a warning, staring at Ruth until finally she got the hint and relented. I'll call you girls in a bit. Out! Out! Right this instant.

Turn it up, Courtney said in the den. Quick.

You, said Paige. But when the voices got louder in the kitchen, she threw Courtney the remote.

They lay low together on the sofa. On the television, a triple homicide and not a single suspect so far. The detectives were stumped. Courtney couldn't follow the story.

Of the three boys still left in the orchard, the ones who hadn't graduated last year, Courtney preferred the youngest, Eddie, with the leaky-blue-pen girlish lips. He was in the other sixth-grade class. On the playground, if she kept very still she could feel him watching her from within the clump of boys who shuffled around under the basketball hoop. The dark head of probably Eddie turned slightly toward her. She could feel it. Like an arrow. A dart.

She asked Paige, casually, through the veil of the loud TV, she was just wondering, if Eddie had ever said much about her.

About who? asked Paige, her head turning sideways, ready, for once, to give a straight answer. Who do you mean?

Courtney waited a moment. Paige was teasing her. Then she realized, no, she wasn't. She hadn't heard her. Well, I mean, does he mention Fiona Murphy? asked Courtney.

Not a prayer, snorted Paige. Good one.

In a little while, Ruth appeared in the door then closed it behind her. Turn that down, will you?

Courtney pushed the mute.

Set up the TV trays and I'll bring in sandwiches. She was talking to them as if they were all at the Beach Club. And they were just another pair of snotty kids waiting for their fries.

The following Monday, Mr. Kemp from the orchard called Ruth on the telephone with terrible, shocking news about Paige. News that Ruth could scarcely believe much less repeat. Now Paige was the one sitting at the kitchen table waiting for justice. And Courtney was curled up on the sofa in the den still in her school uniform, eyes half-closed, watching a western. The long ruffled dresses on the saloon girls, the spark in their attitude, smiling for the deputy, who was a dunce, and longing for the sheriff, who was not. *Bang, bang, bang*, the crooked guys were run out of town. Most of them near dead. Now Paige was listening to Ruth's threats, rehearsing what their father would say when he knew what she'd been doing in Mr. Kemp's good clean orchard. People eat those apples!

Ruth was bug-eyed with excitement. And something in her enthusiasm, the lush happiness of it, made Courtney feel that she'd told on Paige herself. Maybe she had. For so long later she would still feel the mistake in her heart, as if she had carried a mean little boy there, someone who would take aim at Paige and harm her, hope for the worst. Over and over and over until she was dead.

During the commercial, Courtney made a casual trip to the kitchen for some milk. But Paige wouldn't meet her eye. Outside in the yard, the holly bushes caught the first pink rays before the sunset. The phone rang, and their father's voice spilled out of the receiver held close to Ruth's ear.

Right away, Ruth said.

She punched the receiver back on the wall, rummaged in her purse for the car keys, and headed for the garage. Now Paige caught Courtney's eye. Ruth? called Courtney.

What now? said Ruth. She looked frantic.

Should we come with you? You don't want Paige out of your sight, remember?

Oh, Christ in heaven!

Should we get in the car?

Come, she said. Come on. Hurry up!

So many important-looking black cars already lined up along Ocean Avenue it looked like a funeral. A whole gang of policemen lounged at the gate of the ocean house between the cypress trees. Ruth knew her rights, she said, but the police did not agree. Besides, who were the little girls? This was no place for children. Someone might get hurt. Already the bulldozers were aimed at the turret side of the house.

This is illegal, said Ruth, which made the policemen smile.

Such an enormous house and it took no time to come tumbling down. The rot through and through, said a fireman later, smoking a cigar, stale and sour by the smell of it. He'd taken it upon himself to guard Ruth and the girls from harm. In the end they were allowed to stand just inside the old gate once Ruth had convinced them that the girls were the rightful owners. It was their mother's house, she said. And there was a sheepish squint of recognition in the fireman as he looked first at Paige then less certainly at Courtney. All right, he said.

Then a fireman with black hair swirling on his forearms came over and explained the methodology to Ruth. Turning his face close to the cypress and out of the wind. Basically I could have knocked it over with my fist, he said. So we didn't need a lot of fancy machinery. Before the sky was fully dark the house lay tucked inside its foundation.

Ruth had some old red cocktail napkins stuffed into her capri pant pockets. Here, she said to the girls, gesturing to their noses, and she did the same herself. The wind off the ocean had shifted and caught up the debris dust from the house like spray and a contaminated wet breeze now prickled their skin.

Oh, you know what? said Paige. I forgot to tell you, her eyes serious over the mask of the red cocktail napkin. Eddie asked me to give you a message.

Courtney looked at her.

He said to tell you, no offense, but you stink like dog farts.

Courtney looked back to the jetty. Completely visible now where the house had once been. So surprising how small and crumbling it was without the house to protect it.

That was the last of the ocean house, a collapse of rubble in a deep pit, doused by spray coming across the rocks. For good measure the firemen directed their hoses toward any flighty timber. Whatever might be caught up by wind or vandalized was soaked until useless.

Someone said, You'd think they'd want to save those precious windows.

But Ruth shook her head. You start parsing this and that and you're never done.

Does Ruth hate the house? Courtney asked Paige. It's not that, Paige said. It's you. She told Daddy you were the worm in their happy cabbage. She said it's a shame you're not more like me.

You? said Courtney. You? People can just rummage around your underpants whenever they feel like it. This was a lame insult and Courtney tried to think of something better.

But there were shouts and the dousing firemen dropped their hoses and scampered back from the pit just as a leap of flame shot up from the center and died right down, a bit of gas trapped in the line flaring, that's all, but Paige burst out crying. She was suddenly sobbing and couldn't be calmed. They left then, and Ruth put her to bed with an aspirin and a cool towel for her eyes.

Courtney, you bunk in the den tonight, Ruth said. And all night long the tweed nubs of the couch stung at Courtney's cheeks like the flying debris.

Paige didn't recover right away. And the second night of the fever, Courtney went upstairs and found Paige out of the sheets, her nightgown flung up and her legs sprawled. At first Courtney was stunned and then she argued in her mind like a prayer to go forward to help Paige. And her feet obeyed. She touched Paige's arm, which was hot as a dish from the oven. Does it hurt? she asked, and Paige moaned and said no. I'm just burning up. I caught fire.

No, you didn't, said Courtney. You couldn't. We were standing too far away.

I was supposed to, said Paige. And I did.

I think it's only supposed to happen for a short time, then stop.

On the third night, Ruth said, Fever or not, it's time to rejoin the living. And when their father came home it was like the girls were watching a beautiful show. It had nothing to do with them. Paige, pale and sulky in her green pajamas, at the dinner table. Their father was telling Ruth the big news from the courthouse. The town council. His lawyers had finally severed the witch's head.

What head? asked Courtney.

Her father couldn't hear her. That conniving bitch, he said to Ruth. She thought she'd just go on strangling me from hell.

Who?

Sweetheart? their father said to Ruth. Pausing like the sheriff, finally about to choose the right saloon girl, the most virtuous. Sweetheart, they dropped the charges.

Ruth put her hands together and closed her eyes.

What charges? asked Courtney.

And.

And?

He'd been offered a variance to build a tower.

Ruth burst out laughing. No!

Yes.

Now won't those Beach Club pokey-pokes be singing a different tune.

Pokey-pokes? asked their father, delighted. That's cute.

Each apartment in their father's new tower had a balcony with hurricane-resistant glass. This was a big point in the design. So the inhabitants, forty families on the ocean side, could sit in the comfort of their living rooms and not be looking at a steel barricade. They were paying for the view after all. The hurricane glass in standard green was nearly an inch thick and cost one hundred dollars a square foot and would weather any storm. How had the crab-claw etchings and the pale-pink glass roses survived all those years?

The ocean house had been built on rocks, on sand, but the tower required an excavation so deep, so reinforced, it would double as a bomb shelter for the families during the Cold War. Each apartment had access to impermeable individual kiosks like concrete cages with slats in the wall for bunk beds. Most of the families kept junk there, stuff they couldn't fit in the apartment. The oxygen tanks hanging at intervals lost pressure over the years. And despite claims, water seeped in and pooled. When Courtney was fifteen, she led Eddie through the sub-basements as dark and shadowy as the catacombs where the Christian martyrs hid or just waited for death, and she felt the warm silky nub of his bluish penis for the first time there. Her sneakers getting wet. He pushed up hard against her until his heart beat inside the cage of her own chest like love.

OUTCAST

When Lee-Ann first arrived in Long Branch by bus, she hovered on the raised step looking all around her for a signal from someone, the driver, anyone, to go ahead and make her way over to the quaint green canopy the chamber of commerce erected in the summer months.

Get out of the sun, you dope, Faith thought, watching the girl. Redheads burn the quickest. Nearly strawberry blond herself, she knew the trouble a little carelessness could cause. She pulled into the last shaded diagonal at the diner across the street and parked the car. This was all Hadley's idea, and from ample experience Faith knew it was likely to be a bust.

Give the kid a chance. Surprise yourself, he'd laughed at her. Surprise everyone.

She didn't love that he spoke to her this way. But she'd forget about Hadley and go welcome her new au pair. Faith crossed to the bus depot, a soft swing to her gait. The girl was a little heavy in the hips, small bosom. A white crewneck T-shirt did nothing for her, but the striped skirt was good, witty colors, chartreuse and periwinkle, someone's sample sale, well okay. But the girl was blushing, a sun flush already? No, Faith had been spotted and this was the response. Worse than the blush, the girl looked away. As if she hadn't noticed Faith's long stride across the new tar of the parking lot.

What heat! Black vapors seemed to lift up and wrap around her legs. And the smell was thick like something she could bite. She'd worn something easy to cope with, for Lee-Ann to cope with. That's how Faith thought about it. A man's shirt, long shorts, a pair of sneakers, but there was no hiding herself really.

The bus driver shimmied a pink rolling duffel out of the stow space onto the sidewalk and slammed shut the hold. Lee-Ann thanked him, laid the fat pink thing flat, and sat on it like an ottoman. She plucked a cigarette out of one chartreuse pocket. It was a half cigarette, now to be finished. Faith wanted to laugh. Maybe she hadn't been seen after all. As the girl flicked a green plastic lighter close to her face, Faith noticed her hair was wet. Sweat? Definitely darker at the roots, and the smoking hand had intricate henna-colored rings tattooed on every other finger. Great.

The bus closed its doors and rumbled away. The girl closed her eyes and settled into her suitcase in a way that looked an awful lot like a toddler concentrating on a poop. Faith stopped still. She realized the girl was very stoned. Well, that was that.

Hello there, Faith called out. Lee-Ann?

Oh, said the girl, blinking into the sun. Mrs. Barlow?

Um, said Faith, frowning. She noticed the girl's nails were bitten down halfway into the nail bed. Small black swatches of polish on some fingers but not all.

Just like Uncle Hadley told me, the girl said. I thought he was kidding.

Faith wasn't going to take this up. She was trying to decide how best to turn the girl right around and ship her back to "Uncle" Hadley. Did she have an obligation to feed her first? No. Pay her a little something and goodbye, she thought. The girl could feed herself.

I'm sorry, Faith began.

Don't be. I just got here. The girl stretched plump arms over her head in a yawn, she rubbed at her damp scalp. She was smiling but poked a black nail toward her pale eyelashes, and Faith could see tears. She'd been crying. Best not to ask, Faith decided and squinted toward the ticket window.

Do you have a cat? said the girl.

Pardon me?

Mine ate my flip-flop. Some toxin stuck in the treads. I just know it. My landlord's one of those pricks who's out spraying the corridors in the middle of the night. So you know? You go down to do a little laundry and poof, you're covered in something life-threatening.

I thought you lived with your stepbrother and his wife.

Yeah, well, it's their bad situation, too. I do the laundry. That's my task, chore, beat of burden, she nodded. I'm a good folder. I have technique.

Is he all right? asked Faith.

Who?

Your cat.

Ah. No.

Faith wasn't sure how she felt about cats. Actually she was sure. She didn't like them but forming opinions against animals seemed a waste of energy. Like this conversation. It was so hot here. She flicked open her bag and hunted for her watch. She didn't like the feel of it in the summertime, weighing down her wrist. The kids would be done with swim class soon. At least Cece would be. Connor just flopped around on wings in the baby pool until class was done. And Bernadette, her housekeeper, would want to be getting home. Bernadette didn't much care for the Beach Club and who could blame her. But it wasn't like Faith made her wear a uniform. Mrs. Barlow, she'd said, you just need a white girl sitting at that pool. I'm telling you.

And Bernadette was right. Faith knew that. It was sort of unbelievable in this day and age, but Bernadette would just have to stay on double duty a little longer. Faith considered how to sweeten this proposition. Simple. Money. Though she already felt Bernadette was overpaid. She better go pick them up. They could still have lobster for dinner. The big welcome dinner, even if it would now be only for the kids.

Look, said Faith. Lee-Ann.

The girl glanced around from her pink perch. She had yet to stand, a rudeness that was almost interesting. She looked right then left, as if about to cross a busy street, then she laughed. Trained from birth! My mother had me acting all vigilant even in my stroller.

The mother. Faith sighed. Hadley had given her one or two details, and she hadn't asked for more. Faith sighed again. What's wrong with me? The heat, she thought. The girl leaned to the side of her suitcase and rummaged in the zipper pocket. Check this out, she said, pulling out a Barbie in a thick bikini. The big knit and purl in creepy colors all the mothers cranked out when Faith was little. Even her own mother had been guilty of a boxy handmade outfit or two. It was some kind of desexing mind control.

Your mother's, right? said Faith.

How did you know? The girl looked astonished. She shook her head and stared, and Faith noticed the dull diamond earrings peeking through the strands of her hair. Old-fashioned, each with a little pearl companion on a platinum prong. Had to be the mother's wedding earrings, but Faith would keep this second bit of clairvoyance to herself.

Actually, she had a pair, too. Hers were better, fatter in the prong, thicker pearl. She never wore them, though her mother had been so *pleased* with herself when she produced them on the morning Faith got married. Oh, Mom, Faith said, then she screwed them on. What else could she do. Always, always they got each other dead wrong. Once Faith went to hang a jacket in her mother's coat closet and found a stack of presents she'd given, tagged and waiting for the consignment shop. It was embarrassing, but it didn't change a thing about the gifts she chose.

The girl was coughing now. Quite a hack and one hennaed hand only fluttered in the neighborhood of her face. Smoking, she croaked. Bad habit, just in the middle of quitting. She coughed a bit harder, then spit.

Okay, said Faith. All right. Looking all around her.

The girl pounded on her chest. That's it, my very last, she said and finally rose from her tuft of a duffel bag and extended a hand to Faith, who stared at it. You're sick, Faith said. That's more than a smoker's hack. Have you seen a doctor?

Not really, said the girl. No, she said and stopped something. Faith could feel it, abrupt as a dropped utensil. Lee-Ann wasn't listening anymore. She wasn't tracking the conversation, such as it was. Faith followed her gaze and saw an angular-looking man had arrived on the scrolled ironwork bench under the decorative canopy. The green filtered light turned his dark skin an odd color. The fabric of his trousers was drawn tight over his crotch like a trampoline, and that's where both the girl and Faith were staring. He looked right back at them through mirrored sunglasses, but his glance at Faith was cursory. It was the girl, standing, straightening her crumpled striped skirt, that held his slow-breathing attention. Where had he come from?

Hey, said the girl, with an up nod of her chin, stiff and awkward, as if she'd been chucked. She held the Barbie sideways in her fist.

The man made a slight lip lift of disappointment and looked away. Looked toward the ticket window. That's right, thought Faith. We can't wait to get rid of her. Even the drug dealers were giving her wide berth. But the girl seemed some-how to miss the signal. Hold on, she said. I've got something. And she dug out a quarter and some pennies from the pocket where she'd returned her cigarette stub. Here you go. She went under the canopy and offered this pulsing-looking man her loose change.

He stared up at her, legs wide, arms loose down at his sides like two quiet snakes. That's mighty kind, he said, not moving. You're a regular little saint. I can see that.

No, take it.

Little saint, you done now? You got anything else in the pink party pack of yours?

Not for you.

Not for me. That's a good one. Very good. You tell that Hadley fuck, the next time he sends a fucking party hat to deliver a message: I won't be laughing so hard. He curled his torso over his knees and swung up out of the bench. Get the fuck out of here, he said and started off in a trot. Hear me? he shouted over his shoulder, but he was already halfway around the corner, then out of sight.

Hadley sent a message for that man? said Faith.

The girl looked back at Faith and for a moment couldn't seem to place her. He's a soldier? Like a veteran, she said at last, stifling some kind of giggle or cough. He's down on his luck. I was supposed to bring him some cash and I forgot.

You forgot.

It's bad. I know. But maybe when I get paid I can make it up to him. Uncle Hadley probably knows where he lives, you know. I mean don't you think he probably does? I can just go over there and give it to him. I'll ask Uncle Hadley. Then it'll be okay.

Uncle Hadley knows all sorts of things, said Faith.

The girl squinted up into the sun. I bet this is one of those perseverance things. You know, I think I'm supposed to follow him.

Faith studied the girl, then pulled out her watch again. Bernadette was just going to have to sit tight. In fact, maybe Faith should skip the lobsters, just call down to the club and authorize a snack bar supper. She could make the call from the diner.

Hungry? asked Faith.

Starved, said the girl. I always am. I'm like compensating with my mouth.

What are you compensating for?

It's better not to say, said the girl looking down. You know. And she kept her face tilted romantically, stuck that way until Faith finally laughed.

All right. Faith nodded toward her car. They'd go to the diner, get enough pancakes to make up for anything, and then she'd load her back on the next bus. Another message for Uncle Hadley.

The Long Branch Diner with its sticky turquoise vinyl booths had been Faith's own since childhood. Sundays after Mass her father dropped her off here to wait while he made the rounds, to visit the homebound, he told them. Faith and her brother, Eddie, were favorites with Rita Cohey, the head waitress with the thick black wings of eyeliner painted over her light-green eyes. She kept them in waffles until their father returned. Sometimes Eddie cried. Rita tucked her apron into its band and slid into the booth. She cradled Eddie into her high, thick bosom until he calmed down and pretended to doze off.

Faker, hissed Faith when Rita left to check her station. I'm telling. But she didn't tell. Eddie had enough trouble.

Rita Cohey always claimed they were angels from above when her father strolled in the door, handsome dark eyes finding Rita first. Best kids I know.

No arguments there, said her father. Though the arguments about Eddie between her parents were severe. From the time he could walk—which was late, not like Faith, who was prancing around at nine months—Eddie couldn't please his father to save his life. He'd trail him around the house, fetching a beer, a pencil, a hammer, the paper. Sometimes he'd get swatted across the head for his efforts. Sometimes he'd get a nickel, which he saved in a blue velvet box.

Is Eddie the wrong son? Faith asked her mother. She was seven. Her mother was counting out tins of peanut brittle.

The wrong son? Her mother stopped counting and looked at her. Of course not.

I'm the right daughter.

So it would seem, her mother said, and she didn't look pleased. It was a blister conversation, raised out of the surface of Faith's easy life. The trouble between her brother and her father didn't affect her. Just an electrical current turned up and down in the family. She was the pride and her mother was tired. The rest was school, where she was very good, until she broke her upper arm in eighth grade and Mike McManus tried to lick it better. She called him a rapist and he was suspended. And her breasts pushed up in tiny aching bumps behind her nipples and her hair began to come in between her legs and her father lost his temper. But instead of the hospital Eddie went with his unstitched wounds to visit her mother's long-lost brother in Virginia.

He needs help on the farm, said her father. His wife died.

What farm? said Faith.

After she delivered Eddie—a drive through the night to avoid holiday traffic, her father said—her mother decided to visit a health resort. Your mother needs to lose a little weight, explained her father. Eddie wouldn't return until the beginning of the next school year.

Their first night alone together when dinner wasn't ready her father called her a slut. But Faith knew he didn't know what he was saying. Amnesia, she thought and said, Hey, Papa, let's go to the diner for dinner. Until her mother came home whatever was wrong with him was cured by these diner dinners. Rita Cohey sometimes joined them, wearing deep-pink lipstick, starched blouses with A-line skirts. Faith preferred her in uniform, but she slipped in next to her father, just as she'd done with Eddie, and it worked fine.

Now Faith hadn't seen Rita Cohey since her father's funeral, when to everyone's embarrassment, she wailed in a back pew, eyeliner running in crazy squiggles down her swollen cheeks. Poor woman, said her mother. But it was Eddie, already half-bald and only twenty, who slid into the pew and held her hand.

The Long Branch Diner had new owners, but nothing much had changed. When her children tried Faith's patience, this is where she brought them. Now, the working lunch crowd was long gone, and a small woman with a fluff of frosted bangs and a tight skinny braid hanging down between her shoulder blades swabbed at the tabletops with a washrag. Her blue nylon dress damp beneath her underarms. The air conditioner roared without cooling much. Faith had seen her a million times but didn't know her name. No tag. She winked as Faith showed the girl to her usual booth, the children's booth.

The girl slid in facing the front door, and her thighs stuck and made a rude sound in the unsticking. Now that she knew she was shipping her back, Faith was amused rather than appalled. It was an adventure. She was shaping the story for lunch at the Beach Club tomorrow, because now she'd have to go herself. Give Bernadette a breather. Yes, this would be good: the tattooed fingers, the half cigarette, the spitting, the bronchial cough, the flirting with drug dealers. Faith was smiling. My first au pair. If only Courtney Ruddy were back in town.

You like it here, said the girl. You look right at home.

You could say that. I was a big feature here as a child.

I guess you're probably a big feature wherever.

Oh. Well. I don't know about that, said Faith with a smile.

Oh, yeah, Uncle Hadley told me. The air sucked right out of every perfectly good room.

Excuse me?

Larger than life. Everybody breathless to see you.

Faith frowned. Tell me about yourself.

I think Hadley's in love with you. Just in the tragic, my brother got the pie way, you know?

I really don't.

The girl smoothed down into a triangle a napkin pulled from the dispenser, careful, thoughtful folds, pressing down with the weight of a fist like a two-year-old on each crease. Made sense, Faith guessed. Isn't that the whole thing? A mother skips and everything stops in the child, like a fossil. Like Faith had been looking at the gestures, the squats, the noises this kid was making as a toddler, the parts of her that had just stopped still. Fascinating really. It must be what held Hadley's attention. That combined with all the bubble-letter sexual telegraphing. But telegraphing what? A chaotic willingness. It was just like him, now that she thought about it. He was such a mess. She felt a general family policy forming: less of Hadley, much less of Hadley for them all. She'd talk it over with Owen next time he was home.

So, Hadley mentioned your interest in finance? said Faith. I was an economics major in college myself.

Yeah, but you dropped out, right? Hadley's showing you as all triumph and adversity.

I wouldn't say I dropped out. My father was sick.

But you left?

Sure, right away. Packed, went to the bursar, all myself. My mother was never any good with that sort of thing.

What sort of thing.

Oh money, business. She liked to label things. She liked to wipe clean the jars and cans in the pantry. But forget about money. My father did all that. Always. Hard to imagine that now, I suppose.

Not at all, my mother was the exact same way, I mean with money. Never entered her mind. At least that's my guess. Uncle Hadley says I'm intuitive. And that I have the back of a great artist.

The back?

Not my naked back, of course. Just some kind of shoulder shape, who knows. The girl coughed then snorted water from the glass up through her nose and choked, then plunged the triangle napkin up one nostril.

What are you doing?

It's a cleanse.

Faith felt nauseated. She had small tolerance for physical humor. That's *really* disgusting, she said. How *old* are you?

Fifteen. Rounding up. What's your column called again? Hadley showed me. Succubus?

Faith nodded. Waited for her stomach to calm down, then gave her sweetest smile. Sure Success. Socially Responsible Investment Strategies, basically geared toward stay-at-home moms.

Like you.

Like me. But tell me about *you*, Lee-Ann. Really, I want to know.

You mean my own experience? My thoughts about childhood from a kind of retrospective view?

Faith nodded.

Like Uncle Hadley does. He talks crazy shit, but it's tucked into poetry or history. I learn so much. Is your husband like that, too?

My husband?

Yeah, you have one, right? Unless old Hadley's hallucinating. Flashing himself a brother. A straight, tough brother with an unhappy relationship to his flow.

His flow?

You're doing the myna bird thing that drives my steps really crazy.

Faith sat back in the booth and watched the girl pile the wet napkins on the table. She was done with the nostril cleansing, and she'd wiped clean the backs of her hands and her inner wrists. Mad, completely mad, thought Faith. I want to hear all about them, your steps, said Faith.

Maybe. But I'm hungry. One good way to stop the bullshit. Lee-Ann grinned at Faith, perfect very white small round teeth. Excellent orthodontia, excellent dental hygiene. A surprise.

Excuse me? said the girl, waving a hand in front of Faith's eyes. *May* we order?

Faith turned and looked behind her with her brightest smile, suddenly positive Hadley would spring out of the kitchen. He was just waiting for her to do something really laughable, really stupid. That was his whole thing with her. She'd tried to explain it to Owen, but he couldn't hear it. Hadley lived to prove that Owen was saddled with an empty, pretty package. That's what he called her, the package, sometimes the package deal. How's the wrapping, he'd ask. Holding up?

Don't you get it? she'd say to Owen.

He's just playing with you, sweetie. He admires you. He can barely speak when you walk into a room.

It's savage and cruel. Every time he calls, it's a new twist. He's always advancing his next move.

Not possible, said Owen. Hadley's all impulse. *That's* got to be obvious.

How many times had they discussed this? Hadley toyed with their marriage. Whenever he wasn't busy, whenever he wasn't caught up in his con games, she, they, were his hobby.

Ignore him, said Owen. Then he often ended the conversation by ignoring her. And she felt all her beauty, always her best bet with him, yanked right out of her.

For a long time, she'd prayed Hadley would just get bored. Guaranteed, she thought, once the kids were born. But it didn't happen that way. First Cece with her bald head and her scowl. And Hadley loved her, built a filmy ring around her right away before Faith even woke up from all the spinal blocks and brain fog. They'd knocked her from here to next Sunday, her mother cooed, as if that weren't a problem. By the time she could clear the gray glaze from her eyes, baby Cece was wailing in Hadley's clutched, stiff arms, and he wept.

He's more doped up than I am, she told Owen.

With Connor, he was different, and that bothered her, too. Three years later, everything that could go wrong did. Seven months pregnant, she trips in the parking lot of the pharmacy, nearly gets run over by the boy backing out a delivery truck. Her water breaks and worse, she passes out. They load her into the truck because it's running and take her to Emergency. Connor, two pounds, eight ounces, twenty-seven and a half weeks. If she could touch him he would lay head to toe in the palm of her hand. Through the Lucite container he lives in, she watches him move like a stunned fish, small rise and rapid fall in the purple petal dome of his chest. They were not sure. That's what they kept saying to her, to Owen. And this was legal and heartless. Connor's chest fluttered up and down. And Hadley didn't come once, not one time, and though he's the primary nuisance of her life, she will never forgive him.

The full stack of chocolate-chip pecan pancakes arrived, and the girl asked for real maple syrup. Not the corn syrup with the chemical sludge added for color.

I'll take a look-see, said the waitress, and she shimmied the bowl of butter pats in chipped ice closer to Lee-Ann. Just the juice for you, she said to Faith, dropping a curvy glass of grapefruit on the table.

That's right, thanks.

Uncle Hadley said you have eating issues?

Faith snorted a laugh, and when the syrup came back in a suspicious plastic jug, Faith ordered cinnamon toast with extra butter and considered the question settled.

I forget how you met Hadley. Something to do with your stepbrother?

The girl couldn't answer right away because the pancakes were choking her. She chugged down ice water to clear her throat. There, she panted and took another bite. She chewed in such a way that Faith noticed an amalgam filling way in the back. She didn't think kids got those anymore. Cece and Connor were still cavity free.

Your brother, I mean stepbrother? prompted Faith.

No, no, said the girl. My mom.

Your mom knew Hadley?

I think Hadley may be my dad, but he's not admitting it. No one will talk about it. Sort of frustrating, but I look like him, and he gives me money, for school and shit.

This was a fantasy Faith understood. For a moment she wondered if it was a particularly useful one, but it wasn't Faith's responsibility to dispense any home truths between now and the return bus trip. She nodded, poked at the crusts of her cinnamon toast. Smiled at the girl and played with the idea that a chubby redhead with small hazel eyes and the table manners of a cow might be Hadley's own. She laughed out loud. And when Lee-Ann smiled up at her, Faith said, Good toast!

But the girl turned away. Something in the parking lot had caught her attention. Faith couldn't see beyond the table jukebox. Someone there? she asked. The girl looked back and said, When my mom really got in trouble she called Uncle Hadley and, boom, he came over, right away. What does that tell you?

You remember much about your mother?

Completely. Everything. She died later, you know. It wasn't a sure thing at first. They thought it was only a normal punch. But her brain broke. Something dislodged. A chunk of something, Lee-Ann laughed. She had loose marbles, just like me. The girl swatted at the side of her head.

Don't do that, said Faith.

It doesn't hurt. I have like a cement helmet. I grew it, afterward, like some kind of survival of the fittest adaptation. Crazy, huh?

Faith thought so, yes. Do you need anything else?

Like what?

Oh, how about tea?

I'd love to see the beach.

Oh, well, Faith sighed. But the girl was staring out the window again. What's so fascinating out there? Faith shimmied up and craned to see. The man who'd sprinted away was now lounged on the boot of Faith's coupe, working a toothpick into the lock. What's he doing?

Probably just goofing around. No valuables in there, right?

Jesus!

Relax, I'll discuss it.

Wait a minute, said Faith. Don't!

But the girl was already skipping past the waitress. She shoved hard out through the glass door like she would break it with her shoulder.

My daughter's just the same, said the waitress. Blink at her the wrong way and it's the full works.

My daughter? Faith was still standing. My daughter is swimming laps.

She looks like you.

Faith watched the girl with the thick hips and the stringy dirty hair and wanted to laugh. Not in a million years.

Anything else? said the waitress, offended.

I'm sorry, said Faith, not sure what for. She's, well, she came to work for me.

Very nice, said the waitress with a recouping smile. She seems like a nice girl.

Faith watched the man slump farther down the trunk of her car. His weight might dent the metal. It was possible. The girl was doing all the talking, making a sinuous little dance with her hands, her face loud and hopeful. Then she slipped her fingers into the chartreuse patch pockets, head down and still like the end of a performance. This was a nightmare, just a nightmare.

Well, *she's* a live wire, laughed the waitress.

Faith looked at the waitress, then gave her the inquisitive smile everyone seemed to love in her. Please tell me your name. It's silly not to know. My kids adore you.

Tania.

Tania, smiled Faith, now a brave smile. I think we may need to contact the police, Tania. Nothing serious, just a drive-by might be in order.

A drive-by?

You know. Faith watched the man do that full-body lean forward, as though he had a slow-moving intestinal cramp. Now he was looking up from that angle into the girl's quiet face, studying. Faith felt like she could smell the heat of the tarred parking lot from here. Yes, Tania, is there a phone somewhere? Where did the booth go?

To call the police? If I called the police every time my daughter had a boyfriend I didn't like the looks of, she might as well move into the station house, save us both a lot of trouble. That's just Buzzie. He's no worse than the rest of them. You should see his brother.

Is he going to hit her?

Hit her? No, I doubt it.

Faith watched his big hands, Buzzie's hands, splayed across the muscles massed above his knees. He gave a little bounce off the trunk of her car then stood staring up at Faith, as if he'd caught her prying. She glanced away then right back, staring now, too. It was *her* car, *her* au pair.

Buzzie's more a kidder, bark worse than his bite. But the brother, now that's a story no one wants to know.

Let me pay for this.

Sure, said Tania, as one dismissed. She scribbled out some numbers on a pad. Faith handed her a twenty and kept her eyes on the scene outside.

Anything smaller?

Afraid not. Thank you. Thank you, Tania.

You bet.

Faith felt her heart start to speed up. She tucked her straw bag up close around her shoulder and flexed her feet in her low sneakers. She realized it had been weeks since she'd played tennis, and she felt the sluggishness of her muscles. Courtney Ruddy, tennis friend and overachiever, would be back soon from her "world tour" for J. P. Morgan. Wait until she heard about this. Faith waved at Tania, waved away her change, grabbed the pink suitcase, and pushed out through the glass door.

In the parking lot, Buzzie had his head down, listening, and Lee-Ann was whispering something into one of his small scoop ears. His ears were funny on such a big man, high on his close-shaved head and sweet looking, like something she might see on one of Connor's baby-pool friends. This Buzzie was listening so hard his eyes were closed, and he didn't see Faith coming.

Excuse me, she said. She heard herself, heard the tone, the tough don't-try-me voice. But Buzzie didn't seem to hear her, and Lee-Ann kept up the whisper, though a flinch in the shoulder told Faith she was being deliberately ignored.

Excuse me, she said again. You're sitting on my car. Though technically he wasn't any longer, more of a resting stance.

Lee-Ann looked around, startled, and Buzzie opened his eyes and leaned back, just his torso, as if to get a better view of Faith. Something wrong?

Of course there's something wrong, said Faith. Though now that he was asking she was less sure of her rights. You're on my property.

You *own* this place? said Lee-Ann.

This is public, said Buzzie. It's a parking lot. Anyone can come here. Buzzie said this slowly, almost gently, to educate Faith, as if she might not understand the social contract here. But the way he flexed his hands against his thighs, his feet slightly pigeon-toed, alerted Faith to something menacing. It was a move Courtney Ruddy made on the tennis court when she was about to do something aggressive, maybe even cheat.

You're on my car, and you, she said to Lee-Ann, are still on my dime.

Lee-Ann was frowning now, but Faith was replaying the phrase "on my dime." She could already see Hadley's eyebrows shoot up as if she'd said something grotesque. On my dime, she thought. And looking into Lee-Ann's anxious face, she began to tremble. She might have to actually be physical here, step between this Buzzie and the girl. She could already feel herself blocking the danger.

Here you go, Lee-Ann. The man reached into his pocket and pulled out a fold-up corkscrew. Take it.

No, Buzzie, said Lee-Ann.

Take it.

All right, the girl said, accepting a precious gift.

One minute Faith was saving the day, the next she'd been ejected from the parking lot, like they'd magically dumped her back inside the diner. Lee-Ann? she tried. Time to go.

The girl pocketed the corkscrew and nodded to Buzzie, who leaned his big head in close and whispered something. This went on for much too long. Then finally, he stretched and said, Be good, now. And he strolled out of the parking lot without looking around. But Faith kept watching.

What are you doing? said Faith. She heard herself nearly hissing. What do you think you're doing? You *want* to get hurt?

He'd never hurt me.

How do you know? Her voice was sharp, and the people walking by turned to watch. You're a child. You don't know anything. But as she said this, Faith felt it wasn't precisely true. Her brother for instance could gauge the mood of their father by the way he drove in the driveway. If Eddie went sprinting past her room, she'd know her father was in one of his states. Her brother clambered down the back stair and out the pantry window. He was five or six when he started doing this and fairly accurate. Sometimes Courtney Ruddy asked about Eddie because she was nosy and liked to stockpile information.

We're out of touch. Haven't heard from him lately, Faith would smile. She might add a little shrug, smiling again. But Eddie did call her sometimes, his voice as hectic as his footsteps on the back stairs had been. Why couldn't he just calm down? His latest thing—and this was pretty far-fetched—an intervention for their mother. He'd show up, but Faith ought to do all the planning, arrange the surprise.

The *surprise?* she'd said. Surprise, Mom, you're an alcoholic? And maybe not so much Percocet, either. I don't know. What do you think, Dr. Hugh?

Sarcasm is helpful.

I think reality is helpful. You're hallucinating. She likes a Seagram's and Seven now and then. Not fashionable, but no big deal.

There's a word for you.

Sane. Gotta go.

She'd hang up. Then she'd call him right back because, really, he counted on her to be sane. Everyone did, even Hadley. And now this crazy girl he'd sent as a test was kicking her in the shins. Lee-Ann had hefted herself up onto the trunk. She'd adopted Buzzie's stomach cradling crouch and was sobbing. With each ruffled inhale she'd swing a leg toward Faith.

Please stop, said Faith.

The girl pressed her mouth tight and held still. I didn't mean to love him.

Who? Faith sighed, suddenly exhausted. You can't mean Buzzie?

Hadley's friend.

Oh, for godsakes, said Faith. This is too much. Some mobster, I suppose.

No, said the girl, as if this hadn't occurred to her as a possibility. No, he's a painter. But he's got irrational tendencies. That's why Hadley sent me here, to study some clear thinking.

And I'm supposed to cure you?

The girl gave an almost imperceptible nod.

This was Hadley all over, scorning her one day, canonizing her the next. She watched the girl with her nose running, the wet lashes tangled from rubbing. Only kids got their eyelashes in a twist. Faith sighed again. And for no reason whatsoever she was reminded of a clip in an old black-and-white film, of an elephant standing in a river stream with a baby elephant tucked under her big trunk. Faith felt a sweep of tiredness. She should round up the kids and find some kind of supper.

I must be an idiot, Faith said. She touched her damp throat. Her glands felt swollen.

The girl was wiping her nose high on her arm, soiling her white T-shirt.

Stop, stop. Faith reached into her straw bag for a tissue. Come on. No more crying.

The girl took the tissue and made an earnest effort to tidy herself up. And something in that, the sheer impossible cliff she had to climb in Faith's estimation to pull herself together, saddened Faith.

Just tell me. What did Buzzie whisper to you?

When?

Now. A minute ago.

Lee-Ann gave a hard blow into Faith's tissue then peeled it open to examine the greenish contents. Faith felt mildly nauseous. She was definitely coming down with something.

He said: Looks like fucking Hadley-fuck did the human being thing for once in his fuck life? And a few other things, but mainly that. Lee-Ann was nodding toward the train station. The city-bound bus was just pulling in, grinding its pneumatic brakes. The stink of exhaust seemed to float across the street right to them.

I should take my bag, said Lee-Ann. She didn't need Faith to tell her where she was going next.

What else did Buzzie say?

You know. That you were smarter than me and I should watch my stupid self-demolition mouth. Hadley said pretty much the same thing.

Tania the waitress came out of the diner wearing a yellow windbreaker over her uniform and iridescent-blue wraparound glasses. Done for the day. She didn't even glance at them. They didn't exist. That's where Faith's big tip got her.

Hop in, said Faith.

Excuse me?

Kids, sand, waves. Think you can handle that?

Well, I don't know. I mean, how sure can I be? I mean, when you think about it, anyone about anything, right?

Okay, said Faith. She'd show Hadley he couldn't saddle her with a living joke and get away with it. She'd send back a young lady too savvy to even remember his name.

Faith opened the trunk, feeling across its surface first for pressure dents. And listen, no friends visit the house without telling me first. Got it?

The girl dumped the duffel into the spotless trunk with a bang. Faith slipped into the driver's side and started the car while the girl settled beside her. *What was the name of that elephant movie?* she wondered. Hey! she said, glancing over. Fasten your seat belt!

Smoke? Lee-Ann said, fishing around in her patch pocket for the butt. Before Faith could speak, she cried, I'm just fooling with you!

Faith decided to smile, to be hospitable now, and for one half second saw something almost redeemable in the messy blurry profile beside her. Her head was starting to split wide open. *Outcast. Outcast* something. That was the film. A real doozie. But Faith remembered something else now besides the elephants. A late strange perplexing shot of the native girl. She sits shivering on the rocky outcropping just outside a twig hut. The river stretches out below. The rain pounds down. Inside, her lust-maddened lover howls and howls. He's ready for her now. But she just hugs her knees in close with wet arms. She bows her stylish head down low. Telling the viewer that as pretty as she is and as hard as she tries, somehow she's stumbled and there's no turning back. Is that the end? That can't be the end.

At the Beach Club, in the lush early evening pink sunlight, young Pete Hetzler lounges under the green umbrella at the gate. Black mirrored glasses, freckled cheeks, and a puffy sweet mouth just visible beneath the floppy tennis hat he wears. Black sneakers, black socks. A declaration that Andover can't rub away his hellfire edges.

Faith pulls up too close, but he laughs. Hello, Mrs. Barlow. Faith puts the car in park and steps out. Come on! she says to the girl, who seems to be struggling to locate something between her knees.

Pronto, says Faith, but that sounds a bit harsh. Let's find the kids? They're excited to meet you. And finally the girl pushes out of the low car.

This way, Faith sings and notices that Pete Hetzler ignores Lee-Ann. She's invisible to him. He smiles right past Lee-Ann to Faith as he slides into the driver's seat. The girl gathers her hair in one hand and pulls it back as if bracing herself. Triangular pennants clack in the wind at the top of the flagpole. For boats, right? Lee-Ann says to Faith.

Right. But in this case, mostly decorative.

The girl nods, earnest, learning on the job. And now she's got Pete's attention. He too is studying her knees, carefully, slack-jawed.

Pete? Faith calls out. Don't lose the car. I'll be right back.

And just like that, he's restored. She leads the girl under the long awning to the entrance. Faith waves to old Mrs. Ekdahl, guardian of the keyboard, on whom every face of every member—and their parents and grandparents before them—have made their endearing indelible impressions. These days new people upset her. She can be a bit ferocious.

Don't worry, Mrs. Ekdahl, says Faith, soothing, heading off the attack before it erupts. Don't worry! She's with me. She's mine. Just the new Bernadette and perfectly harmless.

THE HEALING ZONE

1.

Connor was still in his crib, an elaborate crib, something with slide bolts between the slats and a mattress made of material astronauts might sleep on. Restorative. Connor was still sleeping in this crib and very tiny when Owen brought home the first airplane. It was gorgeous with sleek wings painted blue as a morning glory and a belly of yellow. Propellers that buzzed incredibly loud, sound amplified by the water, as Owen directed the plane to loop first one way then the other over the cattails out into the channel, watching Connor in his carrier in the grass to see if the baby followed the sound or the colors or the motion. Not yet.

Cece bounced up and down beside her father. Please, she cried. Please, Daddy. And he let her wrap her hands over his and together they flew the little plane back over Connor and landed it sideways, with a crash in the tulip blades. No harm done, declared Owen, and Connor cried—more a *mew-mew*—not because of the plane or the crash. Cece said, He's hungry, Daddy. Cocoa's hungry.

Owen wasn't in love with this nickname. It made him wonder the first time he'd heard it, Faith curling the baby close to her chest, sort of, always a pocket of air for safety sake. Oh little Cocoa bean, she whispered. Funny bean. She stroked with one finger the black down that fell into a widow's peak on the baby's forehead. What a character! she cried. Little Cocoa.

When Connor was born, and this was startling, he looked exactly like his father, a replica but almost too small to survive. He'd lived for two months in the neonatal intensive care and then like a miracle he was home. Owen felt he could cry sometimes, for just the relief of seeing him flex and curl his fist, seeing the funny bud of his mouth purse, a miracle of strength and genius, how much it took for this baby to blink his eyes and strain to see his father watching, laughing, saying, Good boy, little sweetheart. There you are. There you are.

Connor still had a hospital bandage, very professional looking, wrapped around his miniature forearm. A monitor or feeding tube or some apparatus had bored a tiny hole into his arm that failed to heal before they brought him home. On Monday, Faith would travel into the city for a checkup, she'd already alerted the Sheas. Tom Shea would pick her up early and drive her up in his old-fashioned limousine. A Cadillac, one of two he'd bought with his brother, Brendan, in the late seventies, when it was popular to go to dinner and a show in the city and then have one of the Shea brothers circle while disco bouncers were softened up with hundred-dollar bills to let in the couples in blue blazers and good pearls. A laugh for all concerned. Except for the Sheas, who had never charged enough to be cheerful. Besides, they lived, the two men in their forties, with a mother who still had a voice that tripped any decent day directly into irritation. Brendan was nicer than Tom, but Tom was the better driver and knew the city. It was still a good business but not enough apparently to warrant a new fleet. The polished old limos were a nice joke and a pleasant convenience. She'd sip a cup of coffee and hold Connor's toes wrapped in his white cotton socks, belted in the car seat. And the news would be good, for the most part. And the difficult news, a slightly fragile heart, they could live with and help in certain ways. But for now, Connor's face seemed to flicker once or twice with delight, a slight lift of the dark-rose lips as if he could drink that swooping plane his father guided only for his pleasure right out of the sky. And then he was hungry and crying and the plane as light as a butterfly crashed in the mulch. We're all hungry! claimed Owen, and he left the plane tangled in the tulips so he could lift his nearly weightless son in his carrier by the plastic handle and hold his daughter's sticky hand.

Such a wonderful father! said everyone in the neighborhood. Only three houses tucked impossibly along the tidal basin at the tip of Little Rest Road. Now they never would have been allowed to build, but in the early thirties who was looking? Any construction was good construction. And the three houses were placed at angles only determined by how many windows in each could find a water view. The houses were tossed down like a handful of seeds, Faith liked to say, no rhyme or reason. But when they first saw it, she wasn't so blithe. My god, she said to Owen. How is this place even possible? And it wasn't quite possible, but Owen sold the stock that was his inheritance and borrowed money from his brother, Hadley, a disaster waiting to happen, he'd said at the time as a joke, but Faith remembered it later as prophecy.

For a couple of years they slept on a mattress on the floor—like hippies, declared Faith—but Owen always wore a tie, and she herself ironed every garment she wore. A mattress and an iron, what more do we need? They laughed and sat out on the back-porch steps, sun setting orange, bright as foil in the pricker bushes low near the water. But once Cece was conceived they got serious about furniture. Hadley offered a book of Japanese erotic prints delivered by UPS. For the nursery, read the card, with love from Uncle Hadley.

On the night of Connor's first airplane, Faith was attempting an oyster stew. Formula for Connor, hot dog for Cece, but for their triumphant parents, a stew, just like the one Owen and Hadley ate as boys on Middle Island.

This house had been the great compromise. This house made it possible for Owen to lay aside—for a moment—the avalanche of bad ideas that seemed to him to flourish when Faith and her mother were near one another, even briefly. Ten miles apart? How would they all survive? Even small dinners at big absorbing restaurants in New York had failed to diminish the wrapped misery they could generate in a flash. What a pair! Didn't Faith want a new life? Wasn't that the big idea?

What are you talking about? said Faith. A stance she maintained as long as she could, and then she'd sigh. It was very hard.

Hard! Hard? Owen would have been jubilant with relief that she could admit this much, but that possibility had already passed them by.

The house was the glory of their marriage. He felt it every time he turned in between the twin white pines and drove the arc that edged the lily pond and the toolshed and the collapsed barn, a miniature left over from the one farmer who'd planted from here to the Sea Bright Bridge. From the barn, two cypresses, twinned again and spanning the blue gravel, and on the other side his house would reveal itself, a beauty, low and welcoming. He liked the lawn to sweep right down, then the lace fringe of cattails, then the walkout dock, a long slender stretch almost to the buoy marker and the gray-blue, purple-black deep water of the channel. He'd said Paris, a place on Île Saint-Louis! Theirs for the asking, an old company flat, overlooking the Seine. What could be nicer? And Faith had considered it, flew to Paris to meet him, saw the apartment in its listed building with the oval stair.

It smells like tar, she said.

Impossible, he'd laughed and held her. You'd be happy here. The drawing room had windows eight feet high. The bedroom a dark cocoon. Let's do this.

She didn't say no. She just asked him to do her a favor. Back in New York, they drove down to the shore and she showed him the house at its most cunning hour, six on a September evening. And then they had dinner with her mother, Irene, at a place called Hook Line and Sinker. Burgers larger than his hand. Irene suggested a pied-à-terre in the city as well, something functional, for late work nights. You know, she said, sipping a Seagram's on the rocks. Just a little pad for emergencies. I see gray flannel. Very spare, very handsome.

Faith watched his face and opened her mouth wide to bite the burger dripping with cheese and ketchup. Oh, that would be nice, she said, gulping down water, holding out the glass to the passing busboy. More, please. You'd love that, Owen. A sanctuary.

Irene smiled, Faith smiled, and he considered. The following Sunday he looked at the house again and said to the realtor: I'm going to Bangkok. If it's here when I get back, we'll take it. So he flew out the next morning, and when he arrived and called Faith he couldn't reach her, not that day, not the next. No answer for a week. He delayed his homecoming and flew to Hong Kong, ran into an old girlfriend by chance. She said, Why not just live here, darling? Everything is so much easier.

They moved in and met the neighbors, to the left—just visible in the winter through the bare forsythia—Pinky Atterlee and her husband, Ralph. On the right, Mrs. Trainforst and her grown divorced son, Anthony.

A novelist! said Irene with clapping hands. You know that means lots of peace and quiet.

A prediction that turned out to be untrue. Anthony trysted that first summer with a local teenager. First there were loud shouting orgasms in the forsythia that echoed across the water, and then the police became a regular presence until the father finally brought suit and sent the girl away to work off her bad experience on a kibbutz in Israel. Mrs. Trainforst moved to Fishers Island and thereafter let Anthony fend for himself. A decision, Faith learned at the market, locally applauded. After that, the Trainforst house was vacant until the summer Connor was born. Then it was taken by the Cliffords, Natalie and Steve, with their responsible, athletic, brown-haired daughters, Eleanor and Sue.

So that was the house that took him by surprise. He was thinking Paris or Brussels maybe. Not Rome, he'd never get anything done, but instead he took the workingman's house on the Jersey Shore with the white painted porch and the long dock. A dinghy wobbled in the wake, slimy oars left in the locks. Owen would float around along the shoreline, through the cattails, and look at killies under the surface. You'll get bitten alive, Faith would yell from behind a screen door. Come in, idiot. At least put on some spray.

The Clifford girls took charge of the dinghy once they'd settled into their teams and clubs at school. They'd come through the hedge with their bellies and short brown bobs, and soon the dinghy was in dry dock, up on the lawn subjected to Brillo pads and bleach scrubs. After that, the sun would work out the rot that Owen had allowed to penetrate. Cece was in raptures, though they wouldn't let her help. Toxins, Mrs. Barlow, they explained. And Faith agreed. Cece should be worshipful at a distance.

Two summers passed and Connor remained indifferent to the Clifford sisters. Something that amused Owen. Already he had interesting preferences. Connor watched the Cliffords come and go with placid sweetness. Only Bernadette had his passion. He'd burst into cooing burbles at the sight of her car coming down the drive. Bernadette and Cece, Connor's two loves. We might as well be trees, Owen said to Faith.

Don't be an idiot, she'd said. And he was surprised how angry she was. Idiot, he noticed, had replaced sweetheart and honey. He emulated Connor's placid good humor in response. Idiot, she'd say, and Owen would coo at her and open his blue eyes and sigh. It was so exact, so perfect to the lash shadow on his high cheeks that she'd laugh. Christ, she said. Two of you. Let's not speak to him. See if he can find a personality that won't drive everyone crazy.

But they doted on him, loved to watch his face, amazed he'd grown so big now, so nice and round and funny. That he didn't speak didn't worry them. Lots of boys developed language late. Owen's brother, Hadley, who could talk the ear off a rock, hadn't said a word until he was three. From then on he spoke in full sentences, perfect syntax, Owen swore, and Faith believed it. Hadley could be relentless about her turn of phrase. Did you sleep through that semester at Smith? A favorite refrain.

Owen hadn't really loved Faith, he thought, until he spotted the mystery bird in her mother's yard. Later he called it love's messenger. But that was much later and not the kindest telling of the story. Early summer and Faith had invited Owen for a weekend visit down to the shore to meet her mother for the first time. They'd been seeing each other off and on for a few months in the city. Faith had taken a part-time job at an art gallery on Fifty-Seventh Street, behind the front desk. Not far from Owen's office on Fifty-Ninth. He wandered in one day with a big client who bored him. This would be something to do. Look at art. She was delectable, said the gallerist who hired her. Perfect!

Expensive! said her mother. The commute cost more than the salary paid, but it was something.

Later Owen said he'd had a kind of vision in Irene's garden. Almost a religious thing, he said.

Irene's place had become so tidy and verdant, the neighbors slowed their evening walks to view it now. Once her husband died, Irene couldn't stay out of the flower beds. And Owen's first visit happened many summers into that urgent gardening.

Neighbors, Irene's nosy neurotic neighbors, spotting Owen on their evening walk predicted a wedding next spring. Nonsense, said Irene when poor mad Smitty told her. Someone had been predicting a wedding for Faith since she was born, like a magical princess. And just like a princess, she was impossible to please, and now she was nearly twenty-seven. But that morning, Smitty, her nuttiest neighbor, Smitty from

Chestnut Street, had stopped by with this latest forecast and some newly picked currants, translucent and golden and fat. Try one—he'd balanced a plump globe on the tip of a long-nailed finger—just taste. And Irene wiped her hands along her hips and plucked it from him and put it onto her tongue. There was likely a trick here.

Go ahead, said Smitty, and he watched her eyes while the strange bitter unctuous flavor spread.

Very nice, Smitty.

Oh! You kill me.

The questionable currants sat out in the sun in Smitty's little chipped bowl on the back doorstep until evening when they'd turned to a bumpy syrup. What's this? called Faith.

It's for the bird, said Irene.

What bird? said Faith. There were so many.

And Owen lifted his sunglasses to his forehead and squinted up into a leafy magnolia. Right there, he said. Can't you see it, Faith? He could. It wore a little tweed jacket and had a hungry pointy yellow beak. It was very obvious.

Irene smiled at him. A rare smile, he'd learn soon enough. Right you are, my boy. Right you are.

2.

A very different bird, a once-living bird now with bashed-in brains was lying under a holly bush. Brains spilling on the brash copper-colored mulch. Tiny sparkling bugs moving in

spotted sunlight. This was the last thing she should be looking at. Faith almost laughed.

Her first day after, her own brain had been wrapped in white,
foam and gauze, thick and wet with leaking neurotransmit-
ters. This molded helmet had been configured to pad the outrage to her head. The outrage. That was all she could muster
in the way of a thought. Disembodied. No story. Though she
suspected, and this the slowest notion, that eventually Hadley
would turn out to be culpable. Was he driving the car? No.
It's true he wasn't. It was the girl behind the wheel. A poor
driver, no experience. Faith was teaching her how. And where
was Faith? Faith was holding Connor, two years old, but still
so little, in her lap. Faith was laughing out instructions. The
girl had never sat in a driver's seat before, she said. Ever. It
was all so funny.

   We were only circling the drive. That's all. We never
even once pulled out onto the road, not even the little bit, the
apron before the new tar. Just that morning the roller truck
had smoothed it all down. And the stink! And the stillness,
not a breeze. The leaves hanging limp in the trees. No, it was
all between the hedges. Who said this? It must have been the
girl. There were policemen and two ambulances. Faith went
in one, Connor in the other. Cece stayed home with the girl,
who was fine. Not a scratch, Faith heard her say over and over.
Not a scratch, as if it were a miracle. Later she would say she

broke her thumbnail and thrust it forward. Faith remembered this gesture but couldn't think much about it.

Faith cracked the same vertebrae that in Connor broke entirely. In Faith the spinal cord was flirted, an odd expression. In Connor it was bruised, abraded, and in one small crucial area something worse. His head under her chin, spines nestled together, his breaks. Hers bends and flirts.

Sometimes now she turns her head and a pain erases everything in a sheet of white. But she has things, elixirs, to wind that down, to give that shafting annihilating pain a shorter, blunter life. And that's why she's here, now that she can walk, and it's funny because it's a bit of a misunderstanding.

It was the night nurse at the hospital, the burly one with forearms you could sit on who'd done the deed. No one believed Faith. But she, the big heavy woman in the Hello Kitty nursing smock, tapped too many fixers into a fluted cup. She wants to kill me! Faith said. She called me a murderer! The nurse would be trial and jury all on her own.

No one believed any part of this story. No one thought Faith was a murderer, and no one thought the nurse—Hello Kitty?—even existed. And so here she was, thanks to Hadley, walking a curving gravel path through lawn scraped as short as a putting green, urns planted with impatiens in salmon pink, revolting, boring, safe. The gravel composed of round gray stones, no sharp edges, no jarring color. But there, a foot away: a sparrow, dead, its head mashed in and bright black bugs crawled in and out of its eyes, sunlight reflecting on the jittery movement.

Hey! she laughed and laughed again just to hear the word. But the liquid stopper sponge of pain started up in her head tamping it down, putting aside the sound of her own voice. She made a hiss, bending down, looking closer, the beak, a taupe, dulled thing half-open. Oh god, she thought and, dizzy, sat on the gravel. Warm and gritty through her sweatpants, she could feel it, as if she were reading about it happening to someone else in a large book, and the feeling of this gravel was important. Something big would happen next. Lots of the trees—she noticed from this low level—had crotches. Interesting.

Hello, Faith. Hello, dear. She knew just who that was, but the voice passed like an oil slick right over her head.

Here's the truth as it was repeated over and over: the girl hit one thick trunk then backed into the other, not the white pines, but the cypress, both only slightly gouged but now removed, cut down to stumps. That was Owen. All that fresh sunlight was wrecking the lawn, burning the flower beds planted for shade. He said the girl had done so much damage to the trees they couldn't survive. But they'd barely been touched. And Connor so snug in Faith's arms, his dirty hair smelling like onion grass, salty like the ocean and sweet, too, a strawberry. Hey, this is fun, she said. This is fun. Lee-Ann is learning to drive. Tucked into place with a seat belt cradling them both, they were crawling along when the girl coasted into the trees, but the air bag, the thing meant to double protect them in extra-safe blankets of air, released on the first tap so fast it snapped his neck and cracked hers, too.

I could hear it, whispered the girl to the policeman. I could hear the bones break.

The liar.

Irene made a big impression on the staff in the Sunny Creek welcome pod. At the front desk, the athletic blond with green jewel bindi between her eyebrows scanned a clipboard and said that Faith had lawn time; she was taking part in a freedom and fresh-air module. Then tea at four in the healing zone. Irene was most welcome. The girl smiled up at Irene.

I see. This way? she asked, looking to the series of French doors just beyond the white slipcovered armchairs. The girl nodded and smiled. Not the best dentist, thought Irene and swiveled away. Irene had large wing-style white hair now and large blue-tinted sunglasses she never removed in public. Her skin was flawless and pale, stretched over bones that looked fragile and small around the eyes then expanded to a surprisingly heavy jaw. Almost as if it had been replaced and a wrong part had been installed. It gave her the look of a delicate pugilist. Her skirt was hemmed, hand stitched to just below the knee. She wore the sheerest stockings. Irene had come to believe in sling-backs.

One of the Shea brothers, Tom, drove her the long way up from Spring Lake to the little "sanctuary" off the Merritt Parkway in Connecticut. Nothing New Age, she'd insisted. Not that Owen had consulted her. No chanting, she'd said. It will never work. But here was her girl made to walk in pointless circles through shaved-down shrubbery searching for a soul that could hold her. Faith had married a fake man, a make-believe, a charlatan. Maybe when she was better, she'd begin to understand that. But Faith, even Irene suspected, might not be better for a very long time.

And here was Faith now, sitting on the gravel, looking like a lost toddler, not an attendant in sight. Irene was torn between going immediately to the head office and taking a strip off the imbecile in charge or going straight to Faith. With a sigh, she knew it might be more pleasant to beat the tar out of the administrator. Faith, at her best, could be impossible.

Hello? she repeated. Faith, love. Don't sit on the ground. You'll catch cold.

It's August, said Faith. She splayed her ragged-looking hands on the gray gravel, skin puckered and sunburnt, nails a bitten-down mess. Certainly they could have taken better care of her than this. And what about her diet? Faith appeared, well, Irene wouldn't even think the word. Faith's belly was falling over the waistband of her spectacularly unflattering yellow sweatpants. She'd been recuperating here for a little over a month and her beautiful daughter had become a butterball rolling around on the ground.

Irene sighed and looked up all around her. Pretty, she had to admit it, old trees and good ones, none of those trashy maples that cause so many problems. The borders were tidy, already planted for fall, chrysanthemum perky and newly, thickly bedded. She liked to see that. Nothing so grim as a flopping cosmos in August. Strangled and spent, a nightmare. She pulled hers up right after the Fourth of July. Missus! cried Jose. The flowers have been stolen! He still worked for her. And she was grateful. He wasn't skillful. He pruned with a heavy hand. But he'd found her husband's pistol in the wishing well and had the good sense to bring it to her first. So as far as Irene was concerned, Jose had job security, even permanence. It had become a seasonal game for her to undo his damage.

No, these beds were fine, perfect really. These flowers faced a bright future. And the house was good, an old brick Federal, with graceful additions in the nineteenth century. A decent-size veranda, old marble steps led to the wide lawn, and there was something romantic and right proportioned about the glassed greenhouse at the end of a covered walk. But the veranda and the garden were in the main area. The residence where Faith actually lived was a punishment. And given all it was meant to do for her, disturbing. Cinder blocks showed in the hallways. The window wall in Faith's room was painted black! Irene could scarcely believe it. And the communal bathroom. The stalls with the doors removed. She wouldn't think about that at the moment. This had already triggered an ugly fight with Owen. And they all just needed to get along for now.

The place had been a boarding school for about three decades, from the thirties to the sixties. The cinder block confusion was the dormitory built in 1958, the year that Faith was born. Then the school promptly went bankrupt. Irene could imagine why. And all this was part of the pamphlet she'd been given by Owen, who seemed content to warehouse Faith here indefinitely. Very civilized, he'd said. One singing paragraph of history on good paper stock and lots of expensive photography. Elegant smiling women in long white palazzo pants batted blue tennis balls in the sun. But here was Faith in yellow sweats sorting gravel. She'd brought Faith a pair of cotton sundresses, but she'd left them in the car for later. And some ballet flats with festive ribbons. Faith on the veranda. Faith taking tea.

Faith, dear, I brought you some things. Come see. Come up to the porch and then we'll go take a look.

That's not a porch, Mom.

Well, you're right, Irene said. But come on up to whatever it is, the veranda. They have some tea set out and some cookies, but we'll ignore those. Are you playing any tennis? The court looks very nice, though morning glories on the fence?

Mom?

Yes, sweetie.

Is Owen with you?

Owen?

You remember him.

No, he's not. Come have some tea. Come, stand up, Faith. You'll catch cold.

It's boiling. These stones are boiling hot. I can barely touch them. Ouch!

You're acting like a baby, Faith.

Well, that's okay.

Did someone here tell you that? Did someone, I don't know, some mental health professional with plastic glued to their forehead say go ahead and act as badly as you wish? You deserve it?

Of course not, Mom. Faith squinted up at her mother. Nice skirt.

Irene unclasped her white straw purse and looked inside. She closed the clasp, sighed, then blinked up at the sky. She realized this might be a very short visit.

Faith shielded her eyes and watched her mother. The tea looked good?

Yes, said Irene, a sudden smile, her big jaw wide like a banner of happiness. And I hear they do it every day. Every afternoon.

How did you get here?

Mr. Shea.

Oh. Well. Faith poured some gravel into her cupped hand then tossed it down. Okay, she said and edged herself off the ground, slowly as if her skeleton was half-fused in every joint. Oh, she said. I hurt all over.

That will pass.

Will it.

Faith.

Yes?

Let's go have some tea. Then you can open your presents. All right?

Faith had her eye on something up ahead. And Irene looked her over as she'd been doing since the day she was born. Funny, she said.

What's that, Mom? She turned for a moment with a half smile then back to whatever had her attention on the veranda. Irene followed her gaze but only saw a few slumped, pajamaed bodies on cushions and the pleasant shuffle of the serving women, easy and reassuring in pastel uniforms.

Oh, you know, Faith, I was talking to Dottie McMahon.

How's Kenneth doing, Mom?

You remember him?

Of course I do. Don't be silly.

Someone up there you'd like to avoid? Irene tipped her chin toward the veranda.

No, no, not a bit. I'm just wondering about Kenneth.

Well, Dottie is hopeless.

Why?

He's been hospitalized for six weeks and still not a word about his release. And it's not like they've been able to do anything.

Oh, poor Dottie, poor Kenneth. I'm sorry.

Are you?

On the top step, Faith nodded toward a dark-skinned man at the far corner table, who smiled at her. He wore a big loose pink shirt with a Nehru collar and the same yellow sweatpants as Faith. His black baseball cap said PORN STAR in white letters. Faith waved, then turned back to Irene, saying, Kenneth has had a terrible time.

That's right, Faith. He really has. And Dottie is just picking herself up every single morning and living for those kids.

I'm sure.

One of the uniformed women offered the man in the pink shirt some tea cakes. He seemed to be sniffing the various icings. He shooed away the tray, then grabbed the free hand of the woman and nipped her finger with his big front teeth. Oh! she cried out laughing. You stop your games now, Mr. Bud.

Let's steer clear of Mr. Bud, whispered Irene.

Oh, he's an angel. I wanted to introduce you.

Maybe later. Here's a nice spot, shady.

I'd like some sun.

Don't be silly, Faith.

They settled down into the wicker settee. Anyway, Irene said. Dottie is beside herself.

Faith didn't seem to be paying attention. She was smoothing the heavy yellow cotton over her thighs as if it were chiffon. She still had a nice shape to her wrists, no puffiness there at least, but she hadn't shaved her ankles in some time.

Dottie said she just doesn't get it.

What's that, Mom?

Well. You. I tried to explain that you just needed a rest.

Um.

And Dottie said, A rest? Kenneth hasn't had a rest in years.

Faith frowned as if Irene were speaking a language she knew but hadn't practiced in a while.

Kenneth can't sleep? she said.

Kenneth is too sick to sleep, said Irene. Kenneth would love the luxury of being able to go someplace where avoiding life and the basics of grooming was considered a cure. The minute he can sit up without assistance, he'll be straight home. Dottie said he won't even stop to say goodbye to those hardworking doctors. But you know those two. Can't get enough of each other.

Faith closed her eyes. She tipped over a bit toward the arm of the settee and sighed. In the shadow, it looked to Irene that Faith was the same girl who'd won the algebra prize then got German measles and missed the ceremony. Always missing the show, that was her girl all right. Faith opened her eyes and watched as the man in the Nehru shirt and porn star cap stood. He moved with an odd wriggle, like a very round snake charmer, and when Faith saw him moving in that slithery way, she laughed. He bowed, and then he skipped down the marble steps to the lawn.

He lives right across the hall from me, said Faith. His actual name is Coconut Bud. When he can't sleep, he lets me sing to him. He's taught me his childhood songs. So sweet!

That man sleeps across from you?

Mr. Bud on the lawn swirled his hips. Now he moved like a very young hula dancer—unsure, warming up—and Faith laughed with something close to delight.

Have you spoken to Owen today?

Owen?

Yes, Faith. Owen.

Only on Sundays. How about you?

I call to see how Cece is doing. He always tells me the same thing.

And what's that?

Irene turned her whole torso toward her daughter. Why don't you already know, Faith? What's wrong with you?

Faith squeezed her eyes shut then opened them wide. She shook her head and yawned. I'm hungry. That's all, she said.

Mr. Bud attempted a headstand right in the middle of the new bed of chrysanthemums. He lost his hat and tumbled over flat to collect it, ruining everything. Oh, look! cried Faith, laughing.

Yes, I see.

Honestly, he's the best thing going here. Oh, Mr. Bud.

I see that, said Irene, nodding. I really do.

So, what did you bring, Mom? What's my present?

Yes. That's right. That's right, Faith. Your present. And Irene found she'd already decided. Very fast for her, she usually liked to mull things over for weeks. See all sides. For instance, when Jose had appeared on her back doorstep with the pistol it took her a very long time to understand it was loaded. Really almost impossible to believe. Even when he showed her the bullets. First nestled in the chamber and then, like a magic trick, in the palm of his hand. But here in the healing zone she was operating faster than a jet plane. Transportation, she said.

No. Really?

Yes, Faith, yes. Finish your tea.

We can just do that? Have you asked?

Asked? Come now, Faith. Drink up. Then we'll pack your things, quick as a bunny. Quick as a bunny!

I don't know, Mom.

Mr. Bud was being escorted out of the flower beds directly back to the dormitory building for a reflective break by two unsmiling men in matching polo shirts. Faith watched Mr. Bud's face to make sure he wasn't crying, as he often did when his tricks went haywire. But he laughed at something instead. He laughed very loud, and then he waved at her: Goodbye! Goodbye, my friend. Goodbye! At least that's what Faith believed he was doing. She knew Mr. Bud could be very intuitive. Goodbye, darling Faith! he might be saying, even advising. He'd taught her more than one song to sing in the night. It's important, he'd said, to know more than one.

Listen. You stay put, said Irene. And Faith watched her mother toddle off across the flagstones. Her sling-backs were taupe colored, just like the sparrow's open beak. Faith's sweatpants were yellow like, like nothing real. Stay put! She watched her mother coast through the French doors, then she accepted a whole plate of frosted cookies from the passing attendant. Seven cookies. A lucky number.

Faith was surprised she was allowed to wear the sweatpants home. They don't need them. Believe me, said Irene. Then she settled deep into the back of the Sheas' slightly better car and closed her eyes. She reached up and took off her blue sunglasses and placed them folded on her lap, as if taking off a defensive headgear. The victorious gesture or its equivalent Faith had been clocking and resisting forever. But she didn't feel resistance now. She felt wonder at her mother. And surprise. And intense overwhelming sorrow that flooded in fast, then receded even faster. Faith and Irene, side by side, eyes closed.

HERE YOU ARE

In the few weeks between dropping Cece at college for her freshman year—a chaos best left in the past—and Parents Weekend in early October, Faith's mother, Irene, had reverted to the patois of Faith's early childhood. French conversation LPs playing on a portable record player in the kitchen while her mother cooked. Even as a child, Faith had understood these droning records as an act of self-reinvention. And now, driving up the Taconic to visit Cece, Irene was speaking only in those long-lost phrases. Je m'appelle Paul! Or she was silent. And when she was silent a feeling of thick sadness settled over Faith. Oh, Mom, she said, pleaded. Snap out of it.

Her mother wouldn't snap out of it. Even as they reached the college gates, then followed cheerful red banners until they pulled into a circle drive near Cece's "dorm," one of several temporary modular constructions with the heating/cooling generators grinding away on elevated metal grids, drowning out the chitter of the squirrels. Coucou, said Irene. Bon soir.

The buildings were squat, beige, ugly, industrial looking. As if to offset the blight, tiny red squirrels danced in the orange treetops and of course the finches, gold and purple, dipped to test the seeds in student-made feeders.

Faith sighed. Cece had made better-looking bird feeders in nursery school. Because the college was expanding faster than it could build, Cece had been placed in a "holding" dorm. It was hard not to feel this assignment as a diminishment. A preemptive dismissal—and Cece had only been a student a few weeks! God knows they were paying the tuition rate of highest privilege.

Faith idled. Waiting with the other parents to be directed to a designated parking lot. Irene pulled the passenger visor down, slid open the mirror, and carefully applied a lipstick. Where does she get them? thought Faith. A dense lightless carmine smear first on her long slender mouth and then out beyond the lips to her cheeks on both sides, slowly, purposefully. Mom! said Faith. What— But now an undergrad in a neon apron was leaning down to talk to her. Faith lowered the window and smiled. But he looked right past her to Irene and her triumphant lipstick and the boy hooted. A mean laugh. Faith shut her window on his grinning face and followed the car moving away in front of her. Whatever their instruction was, she would take it, too.

Soon, they were entering a cleared pasture half-filled with other parked cars. Beyond the grass, newly mowed for this parking, there was longer waving grass carved with walking paths. Then in the not-too-far distance, the mountains, and on this day they were actually purple, capped by clotted cream–colored clouds, the sky along the peaks a deep periwinkle blue. The familiar scent of the freshly cut grass. As if a choice had been made to soothe the nervous parents. Somewhere, cows lowed. Birds looped in and out of the long grass in wide arcs. Faith had to concede: the place was a knockout.

Mom, said Faith. Let me look at you.

Ça va? said her mother.

Ça va, said Faith, wetting a tissue with spit, holding her mother's face gently, and dabbing at the stains now deepening at the corners of her mother's mouth. Belle, she said to her mother when she was done. Très, très belle. Faith nodded, smiled, eager for this one day to keep the peace.

Recently her mother had told her an ugly story she disbelieved but couldn't quite forget. Long ago, in the first days of their marriage, Faith's father had decided to rename her mother. This was just one of many tall tales. At Easter, Irene had sat shrunken down over her lamb dinner like a castaway finding food for the first time in weeks. Cece smiled into her lap at her grandmother's appetite. But her odious high school friend Bobbi, a senior crush Cece couldn't outgrow fast enough for Faith, this tinsel-thin girl snickered when Irene took up a whole handful of potato casserole and pushed it into her mouth, half of it landing on the table in a splat on the white damask. Mom, said Faith, rising, but not leaping. This wasn't the first time. Mom, she said, coming over, stroking Irene's shoulder. Hungry?

If it were all one thing, I'd know what to do, she told her brother, Eddie, on the phone the next day. He'd entered a Buddhist monastery in Nova Scotia two years before. Two years and counting she'd said to her old friend Courtney Ruddy. Nothing lasted long for her brother.

How's the drinking? he'd asked.

Really, she said. You could think that thought from here.

What does she want? asked Eddie. What is she saying herself?

Oh, you know. The usual. One day, she'd like to see her mother. Where am I hiding her mother? Why am I hiding her mother? The next day the bridge club is assembling in her living room and she's mixing a decent daiquiri. It's strange.

Sounds like— he began.

Sounds like the dinner gong is ringing in Canada, said Faith. She hung up the phone. He'd call back again soon enough. Or she would.

But then right away she wished she'd told him the whole Easter story. How she'd walked their mother away from the table into the ground-floor guest room where Irene would spend the night. There was a quilted bedspread with lavender-colored blossoms, make-believe flowers with hideous yellow centers. Faith amazed herself by allowing it through the door, but she thought it might comfort her mother to see it. It had been on Faith's childhood bed and she'd held on to it all these years, had it repaired even. Professionally restuffed. Her mother sat down on the very edge of the bed and tidied the skirt of her dress. She straightened her pearls at the base of her throat. She patted the poof of now-sparse, air-spun hair by her right ear. And a whiff of ancient, dusty Chanel No. 19 rose in the faintest tendril. This exact choreography: skirt, throat, hair, scent—repeated her entire life—made Faith's mouth water, but for what?

Mom, what can I get you?

Maybe a brandy? It seemed the daiquiri expert was back.

Faith was only gone a moment, but when she returned her mother was lying flat on the bed and watching the ceiling, unblinking, like a frightened soldier trapped in a lavender field.

What—

He gave me a new name, said her mother. And Faith noticed Irene's knees were trembling very slightly. She put the brandy down and reached a hand to cup the knee closest. Outside the door, far away in the dining room, a burst of laughter. Faith stroked the stockinged calf down to the ankle, calming, calming. You're okay, she said.

He said I had an ugly, common name and he'd give me a new one. Why not? he said. Who could object? I was his problem now. I need. I need. Irene. He could be very unkind.

Who? said Faith.

Her mother gave her a look, then blinked back at the ceiling. I need, she whispered.

That's where your name came from? Faith held her breath then. Oh, come on. She willed a smile. Her mother liked to play little games, lead her down the garden path until she was panting with indignation or grief or confusion. It was a strange trick that fooled her nearly every time. Finally, she'd told Courtney Ruddy just the other day, I'm on to her.

Your father said everyone waves a little flag, flashes a little light. It was how he did his business. Read the flag. Seize the advantage. Remember?

No, I don't, Mom, she said.

It's true.

Okay, what's my flag? said Faith. She was careful to show by tone and expression that this was a test.

Her mother looked at her in a way that told Faith that at least the test would not be one of memory. Irene remembered. But then she seemed to switch gears. She watched Faith's face now as if waiting for a revelation. Cherished, Irene whispered at last and blinked her eyes faster. Then she was frowning up at the ceiling, nearly growling under her breath. I won't have it any other way!

Oh, for godsakes, said Faith. You're making all this up. Come on. Let's get you out of— But her mother had fallen fast asleep. Just like that. Faith pulled up the quilt to cover the now too-slim legs. As she closed the door and wandered toward the laughter, she thought, I need. I need. No. He couldn't have.

All along the walking path from the parking meadow to Cece's temporary dorm there were hand-painted signs, identifying the new indigenous plantings and the historically accurate wildflowers that were now in last bloom. Purple brushes tipped in the breeze over golden grass, other things too. And

Faith would have stopped to look if it hadn't been for the state-issued posters, much bigger and uglier, identifying the ticks and poisonous spiders all around them. She hurried Irene along, as fast as her mother's patent leather pumps could carry her.

Finally they were in the clearing. She took hold of her mother's hand. All around the "dorms" it was busy like a bus terminal, and she didn't want Irene drifting off. Sweet reunions everywhere. As if these kids hadn't seen their parents in decades. Very sweet and all at once she was eager, too, like a joy she could feel rushing down her body, heart to toes. She held tight to Irene and scanned over the heads of the hugging families for her own beautiful child. Because that was the great surprise. At the very last possible moment—or so it seemed to Faith—her daughter had become a beauty. So different from Faith but still quite something. And it felt as if it had happened—she could almost name the day—at the beginning of August. One morning Faith looked up from her checkbook and caught sight of Cece's chestnut hair waving down to the tips of her shoulder blades. She wore a T-shirt—something filthy of course—and a pair of boxer shorts, provenance unknown. And her legs for this one moment did that fawn thing of knocking in toward one another. Her skin, even in the green light of the refrigerator, was achingly pretty, and when she turned to yawn at Faith, her sleep-puffed mouth was like a peony. Clear strong expensive teeth, dark suspicious eyes—her father's—and Faith understood all at once that her daughter was a beauty. Nothing like her, of course—which had been lamented since the day Cece was born—but surprise, something else, and it did surprise her. Her own tenderness about this surprised her. How marvelous, she thought but didn't say, as if this new thing were so fragile and dreamlike it might vanish if she paid attention. She looked back down at her bills and away from her daughter's scanning eyes. Scanning for a fight, but she wouldn't give her one. (Faith had a beauty on her hands. At last.)

But where was Cece now? Surely her particular temp dorm had already disgorged its freshmen? Mom, are you okay? she asked. But Irene was busy sniffing the air. Those cows need more water, she said. And Faith smiled. I'm sure you're right. The cow smell was much stronger here by the temp dorms, or at least Faith ardently hoped that's what they were smelling.

When she and Cece were looking at colleges, Faith had one thought: Smith. Cece could finish the degree she'd missed out on. So how had they ended up here? By accident. They'd driven past the entrance after Cece's sullen dismissal of Faith's only choice and out of curiosity and despair taken a look. Like a shipwrecked voyager finding land at last, Cece brightened, lowered the car window, stuck her head out, and breathed in, gulping. Oh god, oh god, she'd said. So here they were.

And Irene, too, seemed to find the air compelling. She'd closed her eyes now and was taking audible damp-sounding sniffs or sniffles, some combination. Mom, Faith whispered then. Can you help me find Cece? Oh wait! Oh no. There she was.

The freshman fifteen had already settled in around the belly. And hips and face and then some and, and my god, my god, she'd shaved off her beautiful hair. Don't react, Faith counseled herself. But beyond that, she had no more advice.

Cece made her way through the crowd, which parted for her. She was a big girl with a shaved head, and she wore something like a brown clay fist at the base of her throat attached by a leather thong. Other than that, a black T-shirt with obligatory torn sleeves, a pair of man's ocher shorts. These shorts exaggerated her sprawl-legged walk. A disconcerting gait now on a young woman but nothing new. She'd walked that way—like Popeye! unlamented Hadley had often said—since she could stand.

An enormous smile broke across Cece's face when she spotted them. Mommy! Meemaw! And she raised her free arm to wave. Held by the other hand, Faith could now see a boy trailing behind her, a fragile-looking boy. It was a pantomime that made Faith suddenly and deeply angry. How dare she, thought Faith. Then she told herself, again: Don't react. A reedy boy. And maybe it was slightly possible Connor would have grown to look this way. But Faith always imagined someone stronger, which was funny, since he'd been tiny his whole life, so delicate. Faith stared. Then Cece let go of her cruel prop long enough to hug her wobbly grandmother—carefully—and for Faith something quick and brusque. But by now that was more than okay with Faith.

Sebastian? said Cece in a whining tone entirely new to Faith. She wouldn't have allowed it. *Sebastian? Hello?*

This Sebastian stepped forward and offered Faith his fingertips. Briefly, like a cat testing a string, then he wriggled the same hand toward Irene, who blinked up at the boy, openly dismayed. Check, *and* double-check, Captain, he said to Cece, saluting. Then as if further compelled, he turned back to Faith. An immense smile washed over his face as if he suddenly recognized her for who she really was, and she found herself disarmed, repulsed, both. Then he was running away. Slipping through the crowd to find his own family. Hiding, he'd said. He has his own family, said Faith, nodding, as if confirming for everyone a key fact. Actually, said Cece, I'm not sure he does. He's kind of a fantasist.

Faith tried to find him again, to spot his reunion.

So, *actually*, Cece said in the new whine. I'm supposed to drag you two to the chapel. We're already late!

And whose fault was that Faith didn't say. But now Irene beside her was looking intrigued and wide awake. And Faith smiled in spite of herself. Okay. All right, she said. Lead the way.

The chapel was the odd duck of the mostly modernist architecture on this campus, something left behind by the Puritans. It was made entirely of stone, and inside the hush felt, at least for today, tuned to the celestial. Light rushed down through wavy glass like a direct message. Even Faith could feel the uplift, and she was immune, she liked to say. Behind the pulpit, which was really a music stand, stood a large man with a small head and a tonsure haircut. He waited with obvious impatience, directing the freshmen families to one side of a wide center aisle or the other. Arbitrarily it seemed to Faith. As in a Quaker meetinghouse, the two sides faced one another. Light touched down on the heads of families across the way, and in the very back row Faith finally spotted Sebastian. In the same pew, a young woman with a nearly identical face—a sister, obviously—in a blue leather halter dress. And between the two siblings, a mother gazing up at the rafters. Faith looked up, too. A complicated crisscross. Sure. She looked back down. The mother was wearing an obvious wig with deep bronze curls. A very good wig, Faith could see even at a distance, but jokey, too. Sebastian and his sister cozied in toward the mother and they, too, began studying the ceiling. In contrast, Cece seemed to be physically disowning Faith. Her back turned away now so Faith could fully view the unimaginative snake tattoo crawling in blurry green ink up her neck into the bristles of new growth on her shaved scalp and then vanishing. Irene had dozed off. At last the man with the tonsure cleared his throat and spoke: Congratulate yourselves. You have arrived. He had the layered lush resonant voice of an opera singer.

To Faith's surprise, he was replaced immediately by the provost. A woman in steep heels made her way up toward the altar. She wore a white stretchy sheath dress and black hair fell to her shoulders. She gripped both sides of the music stand and looked out at them all with the expression of someone eager to sort out the bad fruit. Her legs were planted firm, no disarming hip-leaning poses here. Muscular legs, quite brown.

She looked fed and sunned and sexed and satisfied. And Faith couldn't help but think of Courtney Ruddy. And worse, in this context, Courtney Ruddy's early and perennial assessment of Cece. It was true that Cece had struggled a bit in middle school. Especially after Owen lost his way home for good. But there had been solutions and Faith had found them. What was hideous and what she remembered now, watching the provost smile with whitened teeth, was the summer Cece had to do intensive remedial work on her reading skills. A sad summer of forced classics for them both. Too much Thomas Hardy. And Courtney Ruddy had let it be known at the Beach Club—because Faith was home reading, reading—that Faith had lost her husband, her brighter child, and was now left alone with the dimwit. A bit of fetid gossip that had of course come back to her. An idea that circled to her even now and still brought tears of fury, of shame. Courtney Ruddy could be a vicious woman, certainly, and Faith knew better than to confide in her. But she had. And occasionally—god help her—she still did.

The provost in the white sheath dress boomed out her expectations for the future. Not only the future of the assembled freshmen (and their financial co-conspirators), but for the world. Now. This very moment. Being prepared for greatness in these new waves of historic change. Tempered. Fortified. Brilliance. Faith looked toward Cece and her cartoon snake. Cece looked back, eyes sleepy. Then she settled low in the pew and played with her fingers like a little girl. And Irene snored quietly. Faith could kill Courtney Ruddy. The provost's voice grew louder and pointed. It was fiercely aimed, but Faith now imagined she could deflect the poison dart, let it veer away from her and all the other trapped parents, up the stone walls, through the rafters, and out the wavy glass windows. Or better, whip around and stab her in her white stretch sheathed heart. But the provost, instead of keeling over dead, was winding up with a smile. As a closing flourish, she flipped her long black hair aside, an intimate sensual gesture very much like someone beckoning for love. Oh! Much too late, thought Faith. Does she have any idea? But after the aggressive bombast, the delight now moving through the woman's fingers of something wonderful and saving coming to her as reward—as her due—touched Faith in spite of herself. This was the lever Courtney Ruddy tapped over and over again: Love me. It's essential. Love me or else. And Faith understood right then that Courtney Ruddy was afraid. Afraid in a way that Faith could never be because she didn't have that lever, that hope of possibility anymore. It had been burned right out of her.

For a place famous for its free-flowing approach to the surfacing of hidden genius—it embarrassed Faith to think Cece signed up for this but here they were—for these free spirits it was a highly structured day: lectures, tours, musical interludes, a swatch of modern dance, above all a demonstration of the integration of desirable real-world skills into the ephemeral on all levels of the college and so on. Lots of artful food, fanciful in form, industrial in flavor. By late afternoon, the sun was casting a magenta glow into the clouds over the violet mountain peaks, and they were all starving. Cece said she knew a local café.

It was only five minutes to the rough roadside eatery, a repurposed farm building in the adjacent hamlet. Fresh hay bales tied in rounds and stacked under black tarps in the parking lot. Once again, Irene was sniffing the air. Watching her, Faith realized they could be turning a corner soon. Her erratic, exasperating, troublesome mother really might be leaving her, if only in fits and starts. The possibility opened heavy in her chest. And Faith shoved it down. Not today.

Inside the barn, Irene settled low into her chair, head craned forward, sniffing, sniffing still. And Faith sighed and studied the handwritten menu. She'd have a black coffee, the tomato soup, maybe a toasted-cheese sandwich for Irene. Local cheese, local bread. And for you, sweetheart? she said to Cece, then she looked up. Cece was staring at her.

What is it? Faith knew this look, but she hadn't seen it in a while. What's the matter?

When Cece was about ten, a bit younger, too. Those delicate years, Hadley would go much too far with the teasing, say things to Cece that had a sting and worse. Often about her appearance, her body, and Owen did nothing. Nothing.

What is it, sweetie? Don't you feel well?

Cece slid her eyes toward her grandmother for a half second then back to Faith.

What?

Irene's eyes were startled wide now. Her craning neck, her open attentive tender gaze riveted by Cece, she began stroking Cece's hand, then reaching up to brush at the shaved neck, the chestnut stubble, to trace with a curled stiff hand the silly green snake. Irene was whispering now. Honey? Can you hear me?

Cece kept her eyes locked on Faith.

There, said Irene. I'm here. I'm here now. Then one side of her seemed to melt a tiny bit toward Cece.

Mom? Faith said, frightened now, too.

But only for a moment. She decided to keep this day, which was almost over, about Cece. And she thought it was a good decision at the time—for Cece—the right decision, but later she'd have to explain it over and over to the doctors, to her brother, most of all to herself. Even Courtney Ruddy would hint she'd been wrong. Very wrong. She'd have to explain again and again what later were called clear signs flashing brightest red and what she'd done. Or hadn't done. Like race to the closest ER. When they did finally reach a hospital late the next morning, only a passing nurse would take pity on her. Happens all the time, she said. We stop seeing them, right? We're just too close. And Faith asked, Your mother? No, no, said the nurse. She's fine.

But Faith did see Irene. And she believed that Irene, as usual, was playing for attention, for the spotlight. It would be the last trait to go, she'd told her brother not that long ago. Irene, star of every show. But it was Cece's day, so Irene couldn't have it. Period.

When are they moving you out of those silly dorms? she asked Cece, nodding, letting her know how they'd be handling this. But Cece didn't catch on. She seemed to freeze, maybe with embarrassment, Faith thought. Freshman year is an impossible time. Cece kept her eyes on Faith as Irene edged in closer, the two of them arm and arm, Irene reaching up again to stroke Cece's head. Irene was silent now. Looking up at Cece with strange devotion. Okay, thought Faith. Okay, she's being a kook. But here we are.

This would be her motto now. Going forward. Here we are. And here. Soon enough they'd gather themselves up and go home to whatever tricks and surprises were coming next. Because Cece needed to be back on campus by nightfall for whatever.

Everyone ready? Faith would pay the check and bring the car around front. You okay for a half minute? she said to Cece. Irene's cheese sandwich was untouched, but Cece had eaten two apple cider donuts and a rice pudding. Irene was dozing, again, nestled against Cece's shoulder. She was often sleepy these days, so Faith missed what should have been clear. And the quiet three-hour drive back to the Jersey Shore would prove to be three hours too many. But for now, Faith went up to the register and when she was finished paying she looked back at the table and caught Cece whispering to the top of Irene's head and from long experience she knew exactly what Cece was saying. She could see the small pink peony mouth clearly shaping the words: I love you. I love you. Faith knew because it was what Cece had always whispered to Hadley. When she was too young to know better and she thought Faith was out of sight.

THE ELIXIR

O f all the tasks her new sister-in-law, Ell, had assigned, the eggshells were the most difficult. The hens laid eggs with thin brown shells with a greenish cast. Annie suggested the fatty mash her mother had favored, stove drippings in the feed, nothing that would cost anything, to thicken the shells. And her sister-in-law said she appreciated the ingenuity. She supposed that's what came from living wherever Annie had been for so long, but on the farm there was a different kind of thinking now and if she watched and listened long enough she'd learn.

One thing Annie understood immediately was that her presence strained the economy of the household. But what else could Ben do but take her in? She heard her brother out in the yard near the pipe pergola he was constructing telling Ell once more that he couldn't have made a different choice. They were speaking outside for a private conversation because Ben was mostly deaf, but he still had a bit of hearing in the left ear. So Ell stood there shouting close to his face though her tone was practical and considerate. She'd give Annie two months past her delivery, then she would need to find work or another home. Ell was being generous, Annie thought, and she was grateful for the kindness.

Still the eggshells stuck to the sink and mingled with the oatmeal scraps in the trap and made a glue, and she'd used up the paper towel roll chasing it all out. When Ell came into the kitchen and saw her clutching the cardboard tube, she sighed and said, I'll take that. It's useful. And Annie understood. She herself was not.

Annie left the kitchen and wandered out toward Ben. She knew not to disturb his work, but she floated near him and caught his eye and he smiled at her with such sweetness it slowed her steps. Some thought that Ben was backward in his mind, and she supposed in some measure it was true. He'd gone to special schools when they were growing up and then no school at all. By the time Annie was in kindergarten, Ben was learning, slowly, what he could do on the farm. Their father never beat him, which was an exception in the household.

Now their father was a stump of his old self. He'd fallen under the tractor in '42 right after Annie left home. Lost the use of one leg and one arm and half his wits to boot, their mother wrote. It mowed the temper right out him, said their mother in a letter begging Annie to come home and try again. And then she died. As if relaxing the need to evade her husband after all that time had stilled her heart. Annie came home for the funeral and then disappeared for good. Gypsy girl, said Ben when she turned up again all these years later. He was so happy to see her. She knew that.

Ell and Annie had already brought their father his break-fast. After the wedding, Ell had the old chicken coop fitted out with a bathroom, flush toilet included, and a wood-burning stove. A rocking chair porch right off the new front door, like it had always been a little tiny house. She spared no expense, she'd told Annie. And their father seemed to like it. He had his big brass bed under the eaves. And a television next to the wood stove. He sat in the easy chair that had been reuphol-stered in something that could be scrubbed clean, because even with his usable arm he was a sloppy eater. He liked to sit in his easy chair and eat the hot donuts Ell made and watch her bend and stretch pulling the sheets up on his bed, tucking them in. She sniffed and gave him a knowing look over her shoulder, and he smiled and then turned to Annie, like she was the snake in their happy grass, and said, Who in hell? Who in their right mind?

And Ell said, Now Papa, using her special voice, the soothing voice that Ben would never hear. She's company. You be sweet to our wandering gal.

Ell needed to make the point, Annie understood. She didn't want Annie getting any thoughts in her head about family and letting her baby grow up here.

On most mornings, Annie would collect the eggs, help make the breakfast, then Ell would carry a tray out to their father, come back after a half hour or so, and supervise the important cleaning of the kitchen. So much happened here now: the sausage making and the jams and jellies, the putting up of vegetables. And Ell was a bit of a self-made apothecary.

She'd invented an elixir that cured a list of ailments. She brewed it in the basement, away from prying eyes. But up in the kitchen the jars were boiled and sealed. Every day, jars were boxed and stacked. The first Saturday of the month, she'd set up a stand by the post office and after an hour, all her goods were sold.

Annie knew just from the smell the central part of Ell's secret recipe was the grain alcohol naturally needed to preserve the herbs and barks. That it was an elixir for those suffering from rheumatism, migraine, women's troubles, rabies, dropsy, and heart, for starters, any manner of skin rash or chest congestion, marital problems or blood ailments, and that its medicinal value trumped even for those who had taken the pledge explained some of its popularity. The town doctor didn't care. Nothing but a bit of old parsley and pine bark, he said. That's my guess. No harm done and quite possibly some good. And Ell took that to be an endorsement. That most of her customers spent Saturday afternoons half-conscious was considered part of the cure.

Annie was five months gone when she arrived at the farm and seven and a half when she started to feel the fluttering pain down low in her belly. It was like something hot and vicious was threading itself through a big vein that traveled from just under her heart to the place where the baby nestled so quiet now. She waited for the tossing and turning that would come. She kept to herself about the needle of pain until one day she was carrying a tray of jars and nearly fell over, shocked by the sting within her.

Put them down. Right now, said Ell. Loud and practical like she was speaking to Ben. Now sit yourself there, and she pointed to the chair by the door. A gathering spot for things going outside. Clear those tools, she said. Sit down so I can see you.

Well, you're nearly blue, said Ell. Look at me. Look me right in the eye.

Annie glanced up, but she was tracking the slithering pain inside. She knew from town gossip that Ell had tried three times to have a baby and each pregnancy had ended abruptly. This was understood as Ben's deficit. A magnificent woman, said the doctor. A cruel irony, he said, and most agreed, though thought he was being a bit poetic. Others thought he was talking about Ell like she was a prize animal needlessly wasted. And now her predicament was considered historical and set. So she made remedies instead and ran an admirable farm with two men who scarcely made up one between them. That the seasonal hands were frightened of her was just as it should be. Can't be too kind and keep things going if you're a woman. Everyone takes advantage given the chance.

Annie tried to calm the baby deep inside as if the baby was upset by her pain, and maybe that was true. Hush now, she thought. Hi-dee-ho, and she didn't really know she'd closed her eyes until Ell was saying in her loud Ben voice: Take a drink of this but drink it slow.

Annie looked at her. Ell's face in the shadow in the kitchen that had once been her mother's looked tender. Like she was ready, as her mother had always been, to nurse a problem away, no matter where it came from. The source isn't my concern, said her mother. You are. So matter of fact. So good. That Annie had still run away and not even fifteen had caused her mother unnecessary heartache, she knew. But in every letter her mother wrote she began by saying: Sweet girl, I understand.

Ell was holding out a cup and saying in her loud patient voice: Don't let this baby tell you what to do. Take a slow long sip, hold it in your mouth, then swallow. Then do it again.

Annie felt her mouth burning and the fumes like tar on a hot day soaking up into her brain and melting it. Ell kept the cup in front of her until it was drained, then she helped her by one arm, gently, as if Annie were their addled father, to the little storeroom off the kitchen she'd cleared out for Annie's cot.

All afternoon and into the evening Annie's body shivered and burned half-dreaming. At midnight she started giving birth and that woke her up.

Please, please, she cried out when she could speak. Call the doctor. But when Ell finally came, sad and slow, she said the doctor couldn't be reached, but there was nothing to worry about. She'd be right back.

Annie tried not to shout out when the pain surged though only Ell could hear her. It was already curbing when Ell pulled up a stool beside her and offered more elixir.

Just water? said Annie. Please, please, I'm so thirsty.

This right here is all you need, said Ell, and in the dark room Annie saw kindness and took the cup.

When she woke up, the daylight filled the window but scarcely lit the room. There was an early spring rain, and Annie could hear Ell shouting to Ben in the kitchen about a double workload. He shouldn't think for one minute this would be the situation for long. And Ben shouted that he understood all that. Annie had always been a good strong girl, and as soon as she was healed—

Don't talk to me about healing, shouted Ell. And the baby mewed in a dresser drawer on the floor. Annie looked down and saw her son in full for the first time. His sealed eyes, his scalp bright red, as if only a moment ago he'd made his way from her. She bent down out of the bed and felt the shock of pain between her legs, a wet howl of pain, but she kept going, holding her breath until her hand could reach his mottled belly. Hi-dee-ho, she whispered. Hi-dee-ho. And she touched his perfect waxy skin.

Ell was right. It took a very long while for Annie to heal from what the doctor said after the fact had been a serious life-threatening situation of the womb. She still wasn't out of danger. And the baby was named Roger for their father one day when Annie was sleeping. And when she awoke she couldn't unstick it. The pastor had stopped in and that was that. Baby Roger was even slower to find his strength. Born early, said the doctor, and to a sickly mother at that.

Ell was eager to offer herself—despite the inconvenience —to feed baby Roger, to take him out into the fresh air and off to the chicken coop to visit his grandfather. She even took him swaddled in an egg basket and sat him on the sales table in front of the post office from the first Saturday morning after he was born. She wore a thick covering apron and a pleased open smile. When her customers peaked in at the tiny face poking out from his new crocheted baby cap and said, My, oh my, Ell sighed and nodded. And when asked his opinion of all this, the doctor shrugged and said something about God's mysterious ways.

But when Ell moved baby Roger up to her room to sleep at night, Annie began to pine and falter. The doctor prescribed a strict diet of blood fortifiers, something to put some color in her cheeks. And Ell gave her the first-made sausages each week. And plenty of her elixir, which the doctor hadn't commented on one way or the other.

Spring finally came in full. The wisteria bloomed outside Annie's window and the lilac buds darkened before the burst. Her window was open to the possible breeze and she heard her father crying out, yelling curses. She sat up to try to catch the words.

Bastard, rat, weasel, freak, forked menace, creepy-crawling slug. Just a howling, hideous maw. Annie couldn't find the sense. The kitchen was quiet, and she put on a robe and pulled herself upright to her feet. Slut. Scum. Demon filth. Why, the sweat from my cock could do better.

Baby Roger was nowhere in the kitchen and Annie was frightened. His dresser drawer with its little nest of blankets was on the chair by the door. Outside the farmyard went still.

There'd been talk in town about what might happen to the farm after the old man died. Though Ell was capable as a subsistence farmer she wasn't an owner, and long ago, the old man had disinherited Ben on principle, and Annie never had any kind of standing. Everyone understood that. So the farm would revert to the town, and there were exciting things that could happen then on all that fertile land. Nearly everyone had a plan. Some smart planting techniques could be tried. New ways to increase production and cut out the usual pests. But best of all, a livestock-processing plant, erected on the stream, away from the town center, would keep all that work local and bring in a wider revenue base than ever before. The town would burst into its rightful rebirth and leave the ranks of the withering behind.

Now, listen, all this progress is inevitable, Ell said to the old man. We can be mowed right down, or we can take matters into our own hands and ride high.

She'd been saying this for a while on a regular basis. Sometimes she would sit on the mussed soured sheets and part her legs and talk about the mighty tax write-off of a meat plant and all the best cuts sure to land first on their table. And if the old man closed his eyes she'd whisper about the one thing that tractor never found, thank the good lord. And he would hop across the room, not bother with any crutch or cane and give her the business she was begging for before

Ben or any other busybody came popping in to the chicken coop looking for wisdom or sympathy.

But now he said Ell was trying to trick him, calling the puling scrap of a baby his seed. I may be slow, and I may be lame, but I'm not Ben, and don't think you can weasel me.

Now, Annie could hear her father call out for her to be his witness. She knew this sound in his voice. Her mother would always meet her halfway in the kitchen garden and say, Go slow, angel, and don't say too much. God's hand right there on your shoulder.

So she'd wind down her gait, lift one heavy foot after another until she was finally in the barn, poor Ben with his head trapped as usual between the stall boards and their father all tired out, saying, Give me your hand, gal. He'd grip her hard and wipe whatever mess was on his palm down the front of her dress like it was a bib she wore for him and his needs. Then he'd walk out of the barn, leaving the door open so she could see to jimmy Ben's head out from between the timbers and help him back into his clothes.

He wasn't born stupid, the doctor said. But he was brought up that way, and it amounts to the same thing. By the time he was five, he couldn't hear the sound of his own name. Except when Annie said, Ben, honey, I'm going to untangle you now and when I do we're going someplace nice. Usually to the creek to bathe. But when she was ready to leave for good, he didn't want to go. She begged him, but he said he'd only weigh her down, and he gave her the money he stole for her bus fare.

Her first day home, she tucked it right back into his pocket. Daddy can't catch you now, she said, smiling in a private way only Ben knew. He could see her smile and returned it, but the hearing he'd once reserved just for her had worn away.

In the kitchen, Annie saw the remains of the breakfast tray Ell had concocted for the old man. Green eggshells clogged the sink, and the batter dripped all down the stove front for the donuts dipped in fresh strawberry jam. The acid smell of the elixir, made hot and freshly spiced like a cider the way he liked it. All this Ell had gathered on a tray and maybe slipped the baby under her arm on the way out and kicked open the screen door.

The old man sat on the chicken coop porch behind a stand of lilac yelling like his pants were on fire. Annie pulled her robe tighter and held the door frame, then the porch post, then imagined a rope in the yard pulling her across, as if her mother were there, holding the other end, saying: There you go, sweet girl, nothing you can't do when you try. And this brought her before Ell and her father and the baby stuck sideways into the crux of his lap.

Now, Daddy, she said. Ell made a nice breakfast I see.

Look what just slimed in, he said, scratching at the back of his neck with his good arm, squeezing the baby in close with his good leg.

Annie pulled on the invisible rope and brought herself up onto the porch. And said something quiet about the lilac, how it burst to life first right here on this spot. Ell said that was always her intention. Put the best things here for the old man. That he'd have the best of everything and first of all. And her father thought about that. And Annie leaned down and put a hand into her father's lap and under the baby's lolling head.

Let me take this old trouble pot out of your way, and like a magician, she plucked him up and away and across her heart and halfway back to the kitchen, while she saw her mother lift her head out of the garden patch. All on the same breath.

She heard Ell say behind her that Annie had lost her own baby and she'd be moving on soon. Annie was grieving, and Ell let her play with baby Roger now and then just to ease the ache. But Annie would be going and then things would go back to normal. Ell promised.

In the kitchen, Annie tucked the baby into the dresser drawer and brought all the little blankets up around his tiny legs. Hi-dee-ho, she sang. Hi-dee-ho. And she looked about for a bit of strawberry jam to dip her finger and give him a special treat. Ell was right again. She would be going soon. As soon as she could rely on her own two legs to carry them, she and baby Roger would leave. Ben had already given her back the bus money.

Annie bent into the icebox for the jam and found it just as the screen door slammed.

What do you need? asked Ell. You didn't get enough to eat?

Plenty, said Annie with a smile as she straightened back up, feeling the pulls inside her as if she'd been remade with staples and pins too big for her. More than enough, she said.

Ell put down the tray on the table next to baby Roger in his dresser drawer. Annie held on to the icebox now, waiting for the pain to rest, then she'd walk. Ell opened the thermos on the tray and looked inside. The old man liked the elixir boiling hot. It worked fastest that way, and one day Ell promised, his crushed leg and withered arm would be brand-new. She looked into the big all-day thermos and steam covered her face.

He says with the warm weather he wants it cool, Ell said. He thinks all that means is I pour this here into a pitcher with ice, but once I boil it, the chemistry only works hot, not cold and that's it. I have to start over fresh. Can't waste it, and she poured the thermos over baby Roger in a quick splash.

Such a shriek, even Ben came running, a shrieking scream. And Annie shocked still only found her sense when Ben opened the door and took the ice from the freezer bin and put it into the drawer, around baby Roger, not on him or he would die of the pain.

Ben carried the drawer out to the truck and Annie crawled inside and together they went to the doctor, who was napping but saw them in his shirtsleeves and did all he could for Roger, all anyone could have, he said, given the case. He let Annie stay on as long as she wanted even if it meant spending the night. Eventually Ben told Annie he'd be needed back at the farm by now, and that was the last time she saw him.

All night and late into the next morning Annie lay on the leather couch in the doctor's private office, baby Roger's dresser drawer tidy and dry with new cotton dish towels stacked like a mattress borrowed from the doctor's wife. And him so tiny and so still. Hi-dee-ho, she said to herself, and her mother answered deep in her mind. Sweet girl. And maybe offered her a different kind of rope? She couldn't quite tell. The doctor's office was full of opportunity.

Outside the door, the doctor talked about the perils of old-fashioned farming and the ways of the past. When the processing plant comes and the all-new technologies, I'll be out of a job. This is the sort of accident my father saw every day.

Now no one wanted the doctor out of work, and they promised he'd still be useful no matter how prosperous the town grew to be. There'd still be your garden-variety illnesses. You wait and see.

As if to prove it, only a few weeks later old Roger passed away in his sleep of something very ordinary, like heart. But on the day after the accident, early that very next morning, while Annie lay on the doctor's leather couch, old Roger appeared in town for the first time in ages wearing a black suit and a long face. He held himself barely upright by a crutch fashioned from a hoe. Those who saw him drag himself out of the car and onto the sidewalk understood he was taking the elixir for his troubles. His head bobbed, and he had the aroma of a man heading for a long restorative nap. His lawyer greeted him right at the door and assisted him inside. Ell sat in the car in her black mourning dress with a bit of green lace scaling the very edge of her collar. Pretty arm swinging out the window, waiting for old Roger to finish up his legal business, tidy up that will. He'd finally come to his senses about who was family and who wasn't. Then he'd hobble back down to ride home with her and take in the glory of the spring day. By September, Ell would break ground on her new processing plant by the stream. She'd divert her seasonal workers from the fields, and although they were unskilled at building they'd get the general idea.

A day or two more on the doctor's sofa and Annie was finally able to walk. The doctor's wife lent her the clothes she needed. Things worn after her own babies were born but they didn't fit anymore. Between patients, the doctor drove Annie to the bus station three towns away and waited with her until it was time to board.

You need me to get any kind of message out to the farm?

She shook her head.

Well, at least you always have a place to come home to, he said. That's a blessing for you.

She nodded.

You'll feel like yourself again soon enough. And she nodded once more, knowing he meant kindness but of a very narrow sort.

On the bus, she found a seat away from the restless eyes of the bus driver in the mirror and the stink of the diesel in the far back. Midway, she sat across from an old lady in a large gray wig with a carton of Lucky Strikes balanced on her lap, carefully, like they were breakable.

Would you like one? she said to Annie in a friendly voice. I'd have to open up the carton.

Don't you bother, Annie said. But thank you.

Heading someplace nice?

I think I need to sleep now, said Annie. She still slept most of the time and wished she could figure out a way to stay that way for good.

You go to visit the lady in front of the P.O. with the tonic? You look like you've had a cure.

Annie kept her eyes closed.

I've heard all about her. She's famous. Ell-son. Ellison. Just Ell.

Short.

I know, said Annie, feeling the surge of sleep begin behind her eyes and pour into her lungs and her belly. Like the liquid pouring over baby Roger and putting him down. She felt her body sink against the thick upholstery. The doctor's wife's big dress loose and itchy. She'd leave it behind next place.

If I had your youth, I'd stay awake. See what's coming next. The old lady swung the carton around like a lasso that could grab all that good youth away. Not like me, she said and did some fiddling with her wig. You put one good foot in front of the other and just see what you see.

And Annie opened her eyes to stare now. She waited. As if the woman might just take off the disguise. As if her mother might reveal herself fully and explain to her, at long last, the meaning of all that had happened and its place in a plan that a shoulder-holding, blessing-giving God might consider fruitful or even possible in his universe. Her mother would finally explain and Annie waited, eyes open, listening for every word.

But the woman's eyes blinked wide in return and rolled in a sudden panic. She pounded hard on her own sternum. The carton of cigarettes flew up out of her hands and Annie called out to the bus driver: Pull over!

She took the woman's hand in her own. Hey now, she said. Hey now. And she felt herself pour right down into the woman's fingertips and disappear. Her mother was nowhere anymore. She knew that. Annie watched for the woman's breath to find its thread and strengthen and when it did, she said, There it is. You've got it now.

After A.P.C.

DOVE

All day long, their mother's husband, Bob, held court in her old study. Sebastian reported this to his sister by phone. He stood in their mother's dressing area watching her down the glass walkway. She was resting now in her favorite part of the house, an octagon-shape addition built right off her bedroom, a room she'd dubbed the space pod.

He's called them all in, said Sebastian to his sister. They're on some kind of rotation system, I think. The loquacious potter is here pretty often.

Who else?

Sticks and stones?

Are they still there?

No. Just Bob in repose.

His sister, Chloe, was on the road from the city. You're taking your sweet time, he said. But softly, then: You're okay. She's tired though, really tired. And talking about a woman who's going to kiss her. Must be Nana.

Chloe said she needed to concentrate on driving. So he got off the line and stood staring at his mother's blue jean shorts hanging on a hook. She wore them in the garden like a teenager. They were just stuck there like spring was going to happen any minute.

That you, Chloe? his mother called out then started coughing.

Sebastian looked around for the nurse, who was supposed to be a constant. That's what Bob said his mother needed now, constant care. He hadn't seen Jemma for at least an hour. Mom? he said going through. You comfortable?

But his mother, startled to see him, began wheezing. She waved at him to do something, but it was hard to know what. She was waving toward the spider plant.

Sebastian went over and clasped her flailing hand. She tore it away from him and slapped at her back. On the floor there was an assortment of yoga toys. She'd been so good at all of that. Limber. And he had the idea that maybe she wanted one. He picked up an orange foam brick and offered it to her. She did stop wheezing and looked at him with a kind of studious bafflement. A quick muted variation on the expression he'd been seeing since he was tiny. He put the brick down and called for Jemma on the monitor.

What the hell? he whispered as Jemma finally rustled into the space pod.

He made his whole body a gesture of exasperation while Jemma eased her big wide hands down Rebecca's back and felt around like she was locating then rearranging the hitch in her lungs. That's it, said Rebecca, finding her breath. That's right.

Then sure enough, he hadn't been so wrong, the orange brick was back. Jemma laid a fat pillow across the wasted thighs, then the brick on top, then eased his mother forward so her head rested there while Jemma did some complicated tapping around her shoulder blades until his mother sighed. Okay, he said. I'll be in the kitchen if you need me.

There was a lot of choreography around comfort, all sorts of poses and tricks, but everyone conceded that Jemma, despite her strange scent—as if she wore a sprig of herbs beneath her smock—was the canniest at getting Rebecca settled.

She has a miraculous sense of touch, Rebecca said to Sebastian when he first arrived, when his mother was still making her standard introductions, her usual checklist of the fabulous.

Jemma has a weird smell, Sebastian reported to Chloe when she called back. Like vegetables.

Where did Jemma come from? asked Chloe.

Bob.

Of course, said Chloe. And then again she needed to be driving not talking.

Are you driving in your parking spot? Like play driving? Even for you this is a slow arrival.

No. I'm driving on the thruway, which is pretty icy actually.

Just get here.

I will, soon. Ciao, Bastard.

Ciao, Clone.

It didn't help, these stupid conversations. Either she was here or she wasn't. And so far, he'd been on his own for days with aromatic Jemma and, of course, Bob.

Sebastian dropped the ancient cordless on the kitchen counter next to the pill bottles and ampules Jemma had arrayed along the soapstone backsplash like a field hospital. If his mother were still moving around she'd have a fit. Hated a cluttered countertop. And soon Jemma would be snapping at him for contaminating the zone. He yanked open the pine plank–covered refrigerator door. Fake *out*! Chloe had shouted at Thanksgiving. Wow. Is this your new idea of country style?

No, their mother had said in a warning whisper. But it is Bob's.

And that quieted them up. Since when was Bob calling the decorating shots? And later Chloe explained, Well, it goes with the territory.

It does?

Sometimes, said Chloe, all mistress of the information. It's weird. You'll understand when you've really met someone.

We're talking about Bob, now, right?

I mean for Mom, yes. It seems we're talking about Bob.

But of course for Chloe all talk led to Karl. Karl of the year-round buttoned-up cuffs, Karl of the monthly haircut in the basement of the Plaza Hotel no matter how broke he was, Karl of the fluttering creepy hand towel business instead of sex and the dirty talk about what he'd do to Chloe once she grew up enough to love him in the way he required.

How's Karl? he asked.

Well? she said. It's a little hard to say.

And the next thing she was huddled up in the study reading Marianne Williamson until Bob announced dinner. At Thanksgiving their mother could still walk to the table, and her hair was growing back in surprising curls, and they'd never heard of Jemma. The worst thing then had been the glue smell from all the new pine paneling in the kitchen and Sebastian's academic suspension from Hampshire College.

How do you get suspended from a school that basically says you can burp and get credit? Only you, Tardo.

Be serious, Chloe, said their mother, who then descended into a cough.

I *am* serious. I don't get it.

How's Karl? asked their mother when she could recover her breath. I'm sorry he couldn't be with us.

Well, he always does the shelter dinner, you know. And then there's a big meeting after and he runs that, too. Holidays are intense there. It's in demand because the food is so much better. Overall.

Privately funded? asked Bob, nodding, like he was saying something meaningful, and not even their mother answered him because she was looking at Chloe. He's so much older, darling, she smiled. You have such different interests. I love what you're doing with your hair. Their mother leaned in to caress Chloe's new bob with the wide white streak.

Are you sizing me up for a wig?

No, honey, their mother laughed. She had a whole collection. I just like it on you. Very in, very vogue.

Chloe's at *Elle*, Mom!

I know, she said, and there was that baffled look.

Chloe was a perma-intern at *Elle*. That's what Karl called her. She made about fourteen cents a week and that was a source of conflict. Right now, on the thruway, Chloe probably had to pull over so she could explain to Karl— again—why she wasn't willing to quit her job yet. That was the delay, Sebastian knew, the long knotty phone calls with Karl about Chloe's deeper self being mowed down by *Elle*'s Beauty Department.

Outside it was starting to snow. His mother had taped a cutout paper snowflake in the big kitchen window just like every Christmas. He thought it might even be the first one she'd ever made, by the rips and the strange, slightly swollen texture of the paper. She did that as an artist. Made a long series of variations, then, surprise, brought back the original for a while. That it hadn't come down yet was a clue to when her illness changed, so fast, from something that hovered over them for years to Jemma.

Sebastian stood close and watched the flakes falling outside in between the cuts his mother had made. The dusk was thickening and whoever was on casserole duty pulled into the drive. The door chimes rang, and Jemma scolded in a whisper as if his mother could no longer tolerate the sound of her own front door. Jemma came into the kitchen lugging a big lasagna pan while the neighbor shuffled head-down back to their car. Visiting time was over.

I'm out of here, he said. He plucked up the phone as he left.

Cradle it, please, said Jemma. We don't want to lose the charge now, do we?

Sebastian shook his head.

That's right.

Like he was four. He had a fast strange sudden urge to hurl the phone at Jemma. But not actually hit her, of course. If only Chloe were here, there'd be some clarity about who was family and who were temps.

But Chloe, as always, was on her way. He carried the phone back down the long gallery full of his mother's paintings toward the master bedroom. The phone cradle was in there somewhere, near the bed, though his mother stayed all the time in the space pod now. Only Bob slept under the canopy he'd built years ago as her wedding gift. Old fish-patterned boxers oozed from under his mother's pristine hemstitch neck pillow. Buff or full pajamas, Chloe had said about a month into the *Elle* gulag. The first of many dictums to come. The phone rang again in his hand.

Cantrell residence, he mumbled. Jemma insisted. So many services were calling, and it saved confusion. She preferred he didn't answer the phone at all.

Tardo. It was Chloe again.

Hey, the commander has me doing things, like tasks.

Well, that's probably for the best. Listen. Karl wants to come up.

Really?

Chloe had a sniffle in her voice. Yes, he thinks it's important that he support me, you know, now.

Well, don't you have a say?

I do and he's got a point. So I'm going to wait for him in Poughkeepsie. He's getting on the train, or he probably already has. Anyway, I won't be that delayed.

Come on.

So listen, go ask Bob if it's okay.

Bob?

Well, yeah, it's his house.

It's Mom's house. It's our house.

Chloe seemed to be listening to something else. Sweetie, she said. Please ask Bob.

Hold on.

Sebastian tossed the receiver on the quilt and went down the glass walkway to the space pod. His mother was restless in her bed. The sides were pulled up for just these times when she tossed around. She'd fallen out more than once and had long frightening bruises on her left thigh that Jemma bathed with cool water and baking soda. She was moving her head back and forth and murmuring: Come here, come here.

Sebastian came closer and touched her shaking hand. Always so graceful, there were two photographs of just her hands in the study because they were so pretty and full of good touch. He put his fingers under her palm as if to siphon off some of that good touch now.

Mama, Chloe wants to bring Karl.

Coming now, she said, but his mother was looking away from him, blinking toward the ficus. She's coming.

Chloe's coming. Yes.

No. No. His mother's eyes flew wide open. No! she shouted.

Then Jemma was hustling in with the full morphine syringe. She tilted his mother's head gently right back like a cat's and squirted. There we go, said Jemma. There we go. And with the release of her grip his mother calmed down.

Let your mother rest now.

Sebastian retrieved the phone buried in the quilt. Mom says *no* to Karl, he said. And then: Chloe? But Chloe was gone. The phone was out of juice.

Maybe he should just get out of the house for a minute. The front door slammed behind him by mistake. He thought Jemma would come running, but he meandered down the driveway uninterrupted. The creek was only half-frozen so far, rumbling over the rocky outcroppings. This was something he usually liked to watch. They all did.

When his mother first bought their house after the divorce, everything was in boxes and looked to stay that way for a while. No one had the heart to unpack. So they spent a lot of time in the meadow, by the creek. His father had just moved all the way to South America though the judge had given him half custody.

Let him, said their mother, angry. Just let him. But her hand cupping his shoulder wasn't angry at all. She didn't hold tight, didn't caress, and he could almost tolerate that. South America. Lima, Peru. One minute his father just wanted a little peace, the next he lived on another continent. Her hand stayed quiet on his shoulder, and an eagle flew up the creek, white head, some white belly feathers, white tail.

It's a dove! he cried out.

And his mother gave that look of hers. Sweetheart? she said. He was only five. He thought dove was a pretty good guess. But it was a joke that lasted forever.

Lately, there was talk of a cell phone tower finally coming into the area, which of course would make the whole phone thing easier. But there were those who felt it would ruin everything perfect here, the rural quality a convenient two hours from Midtown Manhattan.

It's really shocking, said their mother when they first arrived. And it was. They'd missed just about everything about the city. Friends, school, goofball doorman, sour tippler doorman, father. Their mother built her space pod, a glass octagon that took in every inch of sky and land and water. Chloe and Sebastian went to a Country Day School, and then quick as anything Bard honors for Chloe, then the dungeons of *Elle*. Meanwhile Sebastian was still working out the difference between an eagle and a dove. Ha, ha, ha.

Give Bob a hand, his mother said when Sebastian first arrived. She was talking more then. That Chloe should have come much sooner was just a sad fact and now she'd be diluted by Karl, the flaky tyrant.

What does Bob need help with, Mom?

Just the two of them in the space pod and he was slumped in her old silk wing chair, playing dive bombers with the baby spider plants. Crashing the little tendrils into one another. His mother frowned.

It's a project? he said. A video thing I'm working on. This is like the choreography?

She'd laughed at this blatant fabrication. Though it wasn't entirely that. He would come up with something later that used time-lapse footage of small spider plants in violent mangling explosions. It was fascinating and took a whole semester to complete when they finally let him back into school. On pity parole, Chloe would say.

What does Bob need help with, Mom?

She was lying still, eyes closed. Her hair fanned out on the blue pillow. She'd been sweaty and her fragile hair knotted easily, but now Jemma had combed it into a transparent wavy white halo, so angelic it embarrassed him. If his mother knew, she'd scrap this nonsense. Always simple with her appearance.

Mama?

Bob's not strong the way you are, love. You have to let him be a part of things, you know. You can't just jettison him anymore.

Why not? he wondered, but he didn't say this out loud. And his mother opened her eyes and gave him the *essence*.

Chloe had named it when they were young. They must have been bathed in it as babies, but later it was a rare event announced by the recipient and coveted by the listener, back and forth, back and forth. You know I'm not scared, right? she said. And he nodded. Because he did know that.

Now the snow was getting serious, so he turned toward the house and got inside the front door just in time to see Bob running down the long gallery, then running back again to the foyer and waving Sebastian in as if he needed an invitation.

That's right, Bob was saying into the phone. That's right. One-oh-four. I said one-oh-four. *Four.*

Which could only mean his mother had popped one of her high fevers and Bob was flagging the doctor. Sebastian followed Bob. He shook off the old impulse to mimic Bob's lock-kneed walk that Chloe could do perfectly. An affectation, she said, along with the combing of genealogy websites for Puritan forebears. Other than that, Bob was a freelance photographer. Very free, said Chloe.

He has no one but us, their mother had told them solemnly one night just after Christmas.

And Chloe had corrected: Mostly you, Mom. I mean, when you really think about it.

Well, he'll need both of you now, too, she'd said but didn't elaborate. And the idea of Bob needing something from Sebastian felt like a small bad flu.

* * *

In the space pod, his mother's sheets were tangled again from all the commotion. Jemma held a cool washcloth to her forehead. She had a glass of ice nearby to feed little chips into her panting mouth. Take a breath, Rebecca, said Jemma.

No, said his mother, or more a head shake than the word. It hurt too much. It hurt too much. But the cloth was soothing and her breathing began to quiet down, and before the doctor was ringing the chimes instead of coming right in, her fever had already diminished a tiny bit. These spikes didn't mean much the doctor said. He was glad to come out all the same. Let me take a look, since I'm here. And Jemma cleared the room.

Back in his mother's study, Bob had been compiling a list on a joke notepad decorated with a cartoon bumblebee. HONEY-DO was printed on the top. These were the names of the first people they'd need to call, Bob said. He was dividing the names among the three of them.

I'm giving Chloe your aunt Beatrice, said Bob and raised his eyebrows. This gave him the look, oddly, of a saint in a Florentine painting. Images his mother kept tacked up in her studio, especially the blue-faced Madonnas and their practical smiles.

On the desk, Bob had gathered a little pile of photos he planned to make copies of later to give away. Don't touch these, please, said Bob, then left again to check in with the doctor.

Sebastian rifled through the stack for anything incriminating.

As a photographer, Bob's career was launched on a series of chance images taken when he first met Rebecca and her children. Before that he was an artist about town. Also, someone who brought a good eye to the holes in a slate roof or the decayed gingerbread woodwork unspooling along the porch beams. Bob came to fix their bluestone patio and that week snapped a photo of Sebastian, five and naked, climbing out of the creek with a feathery fern sprouting from each armpit. Then rolling in the long grass to solve an itch. Then finally, surprisingly, dead asleep in bright sunshine. Fourteen photographs in all. And thanks to Rebecca, some found a tiny but permanent home in the photo collection of Goldman Sachs. Sebastian at rest in the archives.

Now Bob stood whispering something to Jemma outside the study door in the long gallery. Some of his mother's excellent paintings, the ones that had made her name, were cunningly framed and lit. Bob never spoke of them. They were so good, Sebastian told Chloe when they were young teenagers, that Bob had to shield his eyes just to get into the bedroom and do his duty. Even now, his head cranked away from the display as he alerted Jemma, his whisper voice carrying, that the doctor had decided to stay.

Jemma nodded like she knew that already and Bob had finally caught on. They both ducked back toward the bedroom, and Sebastian realized, his stomach quivering, that he needed to call Chloe and really speed her along. Who, he suddenly wondered, had his father on their honey-do list? Sebastian hadn't spoken to him in years, and like a coward—he thought this, I'm a ridiculous coward—he hoped it was Chloe, because then she could analyze the call with Karl afterward and at least have that little benefit. And just as he was thinking all this, the headlights of Chloe's old Mini Cooper swept up the driveway, Karl's big cube of a head behind the small wheel.

He watched them through his mother's paper snowflake and laughed that she'd placed this so strategically. Like a nice obfuscating screen so not too much reality about who's arriving came through all at once. Break it to me gently. Her favorite thing to say. Whatever was happening with Karl was nicely fragmented, but it was still clear he was out of the car and sinking to the ground in some deep expression of something or other. Chloe stood over him in a white fur vest and skinny jeans, shivering and, from the way she held her hands, pleading with Karl to get up off the ground.

It took nothing for Sebastian to decide he'd just go out there and shame Karl into a little decency, when Jemma started shouting, no whispery commands now. She was actually shouting for him to come immediately.

In many interviews over the years, especially when Sebastian and Chloe were small, their mother said her work meant the world to her but her children mattered more. It made her extremely unpopular in some places. But Sebastian and Chloe believed it to be true and felt they were lucky in this, their belief. Even so, she was likely to forget their particulars, such as food preferences and their teachers' names. They had to admit that Bob kept the details straight. And he was a decent cook. So they'd accepted him as they did the power outages and the mice nesting in the stove as part of their country life. But in a Goldman Sachs newsletter, when Bob's photo of sleeping Sebastian spent a brief tour in a conference room before the naked little boy was sent back to the underground stacks, Bob said his work was all that mattered. Ever.

The last photo of the original fourteen still hung in the kitchen. Again of Sebastian but this time with Chloe, too. Watching television in their mother's study, faces rapt as angels. Chloe on the floor leans into Sebastian's knobby legs and he braids her hair, some complicated weave and snarl that later took their mother a long time to unravel. Sebastian's hands flutter above Chloe's white hair. An eerie light drenches their throats and chins. Karl hated this picture and it had come up more than once in his battle for Chloe's maturity. Her woman's capacity to love that he craved.

Sebastian banged on the glass, hard. But Karl had stretched out flat in the snowy driveway. Christ, Chloe, come on! But she couldn't hear him. The funnel, their mother called Karl. When Chloe's near him, her whole self gets poured right in. Her babyish dopey inadequate self, added Sebastian.

Chloe! he pounded again on the window. But then Jemma was back in the kitchen, grabbing a blue suction bulb in one hand and more morphine in a prefilled syringe in the other. Jemma smelled urgent. Like she'd ratcheted up her aroma, so he'd know she wasn't kidding around. Her scent left a trail that he was bound to follow, down the long gallery to his mother's bedroom, which had become chaotic in the last few minutes, piles of sheets soaked in vomit dragged in, spilled ice. Bob lay flat on the bed, red faced and sloppy with weeping.

Sebastian looked away and drifted down the walkway to the space pod, where it was very quiet. His own feet felt too light to him as he walked closer to the railing of his mother's bed.

Where's the doctor? he asked no one, because Jemma had forgotten something and ran back past him. His mother was very still. All the lights had been lowered, so only a night-light played softly along her jaw. Her mouth was compressed as if annoyed or waiting.

Mama? he said, and her eyes flew open, sharp as bees flying right at him, furious.

You're awake, she said. Go to bed.

Mama? Mom?

Go to sleep, she said. As soon as she comes, I'll sleep, too.

Chloe's here. She's in the driveway.

So stupid, she said. So stupid.

What is? he asked. And her chest rose up, gleaming with sweat, her nightgown soaked through, the linens, too. She arched like something plucked her up from above.

That's four, she said tight in her throat as her body fell back again, eyes wide with surprise. He smiled into her open face. That had always been the warning. They had five counts to get their behavior together. Not one more. Then Chloe came rushing into the space pod, at last.

When the honey-do lists had all been called and Sebastian finally had to dial his father in Lima, his father answered bleary voiced like a drunk, but it was just sleep, just late. Sebastian broke the news and his father didn't speak. No sorry, no anything. He just said merci.

Merci? That's not even Spanish.

What did you expect? said Chloe, whose face looked pinched and pale after soothing Aunt Beatrice. Tardo? Hey. Come on. She smiled. She patted his arm roughly like he was a big dog, then smacked his shoulder, but all that stopped when tearstained Karl stood in the study doorway.

Poor Bob, he said. Poor sad fucker. I told Jemma to just give him something.

Jemma's still here?

We need to pay her, Tardo, if you want her to go home. God, how is this all going to work? I guess I can write a check.

Don't even start, said Karl. He slid down hard into their mother's maple rocker and sat hugging one big knee close to his big chest. It will just ruin us, he said.

Sebastian blinked at the word "ruin." Merci? he said to Karl. And when Chloe scowled at him, he said, Take a walk, Clone?

What's that? said Karl.

Take a walk with me, Chloe? Air? Lungs?

She looked to Karl, who considered, then he nodded in the direction of the foyer, giving permission.

I won't be long, she said and dropped a soft kiss on his pursed mouth.

Out in the driveway, Sebastian tapped Karl's imprint with his toe. Look. He made a snow bunny, he said.

Don't start.

No, it's the money we're not supposed to start with. Good thing I'm here to interpret.

I'm going back inside, she said.

No, don't. Come on. Don't.

They shambled down the sloping drive, out of the circle of the house lights into the dark gray of first morning. Birds were just beginning to call, tentative. Singular. A *zigzag*-sounding whistle, then a short *hoot*.

Maybe we have owls.

Maybe.

Their footsteps crackled hard in their ears. And the cold stung their damp faces.

You know she left him the house, right? said Chloe.

Bob?

Yup. I mean, you know, provisionally. Someday it reverts to us.

What does that even mean?

I don't know. She called a couple of weeks ago and told me. It's his home. That's what she said.

She told *you*?

Chloe shrugged.

Sebastian looked back at the house. The space pod was lit up now like a giant light bulb, which was horrible and wrong. His mother preferred mood lighting. But we can still stay here, right? I don't understand.

I guess we'll just have to see if Bob got the inclusion talk.

Sebastian stared at Chloe. But what if he didn't? Where am I supposed to go?

When she didn't answer, Sebastian looked up at the sky and blinked hard.

Look. That's why Karl's so upset, she said. He thinks it's a real travesty.

He does?

Yes. And now Chloe had a sudden cough. Yes, he does, she said and bent down and grasped her thighs. Her shoulders began to shiver under the white fur vest. She stifled a little choking sound, and then she was shaking.

Clone, come on, hey. Sebastian knocked her shoulder with his elbow. And like an arrow, the shaking started up in him, too. Chloe, he tried to say.

Finally she straightened up and dabbed her inner wrist across her cheeks, then dabbed at his face, too hard. Hay is for summer blonds, remember?

Their mother always liked those kinds of jokes. Weak, fashion oriented. He swatted her hand away.

Chloe took a long slow breath. Anyway.

Anyway?

Anyway, Karl's lawyer is going to comb over the whole situation and figure everything out.

Karl's lawyer? That's ridiculous, Chloe. Karl is a—

Stop it! I don't know. Who knows, she said. And there was the choking sound again. Erupting. Sharp and quick as if he'd hurt her just by talking.

He tried pounding on her back. Wait a second, Chloe. Wait. Hey. What's that over there? He pointed down to the farthest bend in the creek, to the rocky outcropping where the creek split in half. There. Sebastian was pointing up into the dark-gray sky now. Wow!

Chloe put her fists to her eyes and kept very still. Then she slowly opened her fingers and palms and covered her face and tried to steady her breath.

Honestly. I swear.

She slouched in close to him then, as if just to grab the heat. They listened to the water struggle past the rocks. Years later, when they talked about this night, they'd say Sebastian's dove shot straight down the creek, right to them. And then, *flash*, up into the sky. They never mentioned this vision to Karl.

Back at the house, someone had shut off the circle of exterior lights. Though in the kitchen window, like a big TV screen, they could see Bob fingering the wood paneling. What's he doing? asked Sebastian.

Redecorating? Come on. She pushed on the front door. It stuck.

Move, Chloe. Sebastian threw himself up against the door, but it wouldn't give. Jesus. It's locked.

Bob pressed his face to the window looking out but not seeing them. His eyes were bubbles of sadness, red and swollen.

He looks pretty bad, said Sebastian.

Try the bell.

After a long wait, Karl peered out the sidelight. In slowest motion, he unlocked the chain, then the bolt, then the knob. Chloe took Sebastian's hand and then dropped it when the door opened a small crack and Karl glared down at them.

What the— Sebastian said, but Chloe gave him a quick punch in the back.

Thanks, Karl, she said and squeezed past him into the foyer, yawning and stretching.

I thought you'd been kidnapped, said Karl, grim faced.

We're kind of old for that, said Sebastian, blowing on his hands. His fingers ached as he bent to pry off his boots.

Tard? Tell Bob we're back.

I think he can figure that out, Chloe.

Now.

Sebastian slid on his socks into the kitchen, shrugging off his jacket. Bob was staring down at the counter where Jemma, probably, had packed the leftover medicine and the smaller bits of equipment into a Staples box. There was a list there, too, not typed but with handwriting so neat typing was superfluous. Bob's eyes seemed focused just to the left of the list, as if the information was too much to read straight on.

Jemma had pushed all the chairs tight to the table and removed the blue glass grapes his mother always kept there, ironically, in a wicker basket. They were stuck on a high shelf in the pantry closet and Sebastian felt it was important to get them down. I'll get the grapes, he said.

What's that? Bob looked out the window again. Jemma's ride must have gotten lost, he said. It's funny in the dark. The driveway just disappears.

Sebastian thought he might keep the grapes.

Chloe came into the kitchen, still in her vest and boots. She had her enormous handbag tucked up tight under her arm.

Okay, well, she started.

Sebastian looked at her, saw the way her irises had expanded like berries in her light-blue eyes. No, he said.

Bob? She touched his arm very gently. Bob turned, confused, and then reached to pat her face. His hand looked old all of a sudden, the skin slack, the fingers only half extended.

Bob. She smiled at him but didn't look at Sebastian. Bob, Karl has some intakes coming this morning. Some real lulus.

That's all right, honey, Bob said in his new old-man voice.

Chloe, you can't. And Sebastian heard his own voice go in the opposite direction, like a baby crying for Chloe to stop or he'd tell.

We can drop Jemma.

Oh, that's kind of you, said Bob. I know she's tired. She's all set. I gave her a photograph.

Good, said Chloe. Good. She put her free arm around Bob's shoulder and gave him a squeeze with lots of air between her body and his.

I'll probably be back, you know, by tomorrow, I'm sure. And you have my cell. Karl just needs to get going or all hell will—

But Bob wasn't listening anymore. She's off the clock, he said. But she's still busy in there.

He shook his head and wandered out of the kitchen to the space pod to find Jemma.

The chattering birds started up just as the Mini Cooper, now with Chloe in the driver's seat, made an awkward K-turn and then crept down the icy slope of the driveway. Chloe was a lousy driver. And no one had ever explained to Sebastian why the birds did this, got so loud all together for a little while, then went back to normal peeps and trills. It was the kind of thing his mother knew and he had never asked her, because he'd thought there would always be a long grassy carpet of time for that. To get that kind of information. Other stuff always mattered more. But what was that stuff?

Long after the taillights faded, Sebastian pressed his hand up to the glass as Jemma had done in the small back window of the Mini Cooper. And only now, like his mother was still prompting him to courtesy, he raised his hand, too. It left a smudge not far from the paper snowflake, and he could imagine his mother looking at those two things—a greasy print, an old scrap of paper—and thinking about them for a while before Bob came in fussing about the next practical thing and then the next, interrupting her thoughts.

Sebastian rubbed his face. Bob was awfully quiet. He better go take a look. Down the long gallery, he paused at one especially luminescent painting. The one with all the greens. All the greens that shouldn't have any business being on the same canvas but there they were, and the feather strokes inside the boxy planes. That's me, he said out loud, because it was. More portrait than any image Bob had ever cranked out. That's me. And there was Chloe, scattered blues and grays and pinks. How right his mother got things as long as they were going within a frame. And he shivered to see the disloyal thought shove in. Some part of his brain might revolt soon and be willing to think she got some other things very, very wrong. Where the hell was Bob?

Sebastian strolled into the bedroom, an exaggerated slump, pre-irritating Bob who liked a straight posture now and then. But the bedroom was empty and tidy beyond recognition. Bed made, floor vacuumed, all the topsy-turvy chaos had disappeared. Even the gardening blue jean shorts on the hook were gone, and that infuriated him. What's the rush? He headed down the glass walkway to the space pod but slowly now to make the point.

The sun was on a dull winter rise into the tree trunks just along the creek. As his mother had always known this was the first, best place to see that. She'd been a terrible sleeper and would tiptoe out here and wait until dawn, then crawl back into bed to sleep the morning away. Letting Bob get the children off to school. Now Bob sat in her wing chair, embroidered with silky flowers and birds, old-fashioned and left over from the city apartment and all wrong with Bob in his red flannel shirt sitting inside. The hospital bed with the collapsible sides had been folded as much as possible. The floor was still damp, mopped with something that Jemma must have brought with her because the whole room smelled of sage and oregano. Bob had the orange brick on his lap. His old-man hands folded over it, as if to protect it.

Bob's eyes fluttered open when he heard Sebastian. There you are, he said. Up and at 'em. And he began to lunge out of the chair only to cave back in as if pinned down. Sebastian reached out his hand to grab away the brick that was his mother's after all, just as he'd grabbed so many thousands of sandwiches out of Bob's hands feeling every single time that Bob had no right to be offering them.

Sandwiches? Try everything. *He gave you everything*, that small dark disloyal part of his brain piped in. And now it was speaking in his mother's voice, which just made it that much screwier.

Bob reached and gripped Sebastian's outstretched hand with both of his. He closed his eyes again and touched his forehead to their clasp. Then after much too long a time, he finally stood up with a groan and made his way out of the space pod, and Sebastian sagged into the chair and put his cheek against the wing and cried and cried until he was hungry.

THE PITCH

When we heard what happened to you we thought, Wow, that's it. We're making a film. Something that we'll put online that we think could go viral right away because of the topic. You aren't that well known on campus, because you just got here, basically, but the guys, Reed and Peekskill, are ubiquitous. They're also a bit retaliatory.

Not toward you, no, that's over. You can believe us about that. They are known to be always looking for novelty. So this film is inspired by you but not for you in the sense that you are already out of harm's way. Except for the memories, which are probably sketchy, because of the cocktail, right? And we already know about the bruising. We'll be sure to put it in the cartoon.

You are right that this is hardly a laughing matter, but a graphic representation will have a bigger impact than a bunch of talking heads with white backdrops facing a camera talking about Reed and Peekskill like they're pervs in trench coats. You may think that's exactly what they are. But those guys wouldn't be caught dead in a trench coat. Be serious.

You say that clothes are beside the point, except you had trouble finding yours. Have we got that right? Reed and Peekskill were gone when you woke up, and the house you were in was in a town you didn't know. It was dark upstairs. But you followed the noise in just your T-shirt but no bra—that was gone—and a damp towel half-soaked in beer. Downstairs, there were some men speaking a language you didn't understand, playing cards on a lopsided table, screaming to one another. Until you showed up and they went silent. Then one spit in an empty cup and called you a name and you knew what that meant. Have we got the basic choreography?

And you had no idea where you were, right? Well, that's just typical. But the way you got home, if you want to call this crap-hole dorm a home, was pretty ingenious and we'd like to use that in the film.

No, it won't be embarrassing because it's going to be a cartoon. We can even make you a blond. You won't become an "example." And fortunately you're not pregnant. Right? You are? You were? On one try? With Reed? Or Peekskill? You don't know. Wow. You are like the fourth person that's happened to. It's like a brand. Some say it must be a powerful mixed sperm thing, but that's just disgusting. And besides, no one remembers. You remember a little? What's that? We can probably use it for the film. Anything helps.

No, we will not tell your mother. That's crazy talk. Why would we tell your mother? Your mother spends a lot of time cruising the internet for student films about campus shit?

Do you think we'll email her the link and say, Look, almost a Granny?

Hey, don't cry! We don't mean to be casual or harsh. It's just not a rational concern in this situation. We can make you look like a Martian and give you a squeaky machine voice. Especially for the scene when you're stuck inside the store window. That was pretty wild. We can do something with that.

So, did you know you were in an abandoned store when you first saw those guys playing cards or was it really dark in there? Dark. Okay. We might make it a hardware store, kind of a metaphor. You don't care? Okay. Well, what exactly was in the window display? Duct tape rolls, a torn sheet, a stiff dry paintbrush, a glue mousetrap. We are writing this down. All right, we'll make it different. Maybe a pharmacy? Wait. How about a toy store, yes?

So you get shoved into a defunct storefront window by the guy who spit in the cup and called you a whore in a language you didn't understand but that's universal. He shoves you in there, in your T-shirt and the beer-soaked towel. And you're basically stuck there in the glass rectangle.

Were you crying? You threw up. That's right. Everybody does that. It's a reaction to the chemical in the cocktail. They change it up apparently, but the puking is always there at some point, so we'll put it in the film. But we'll make it artful. Maybe the puke will turn to something else, a metamorphosis. So the soulful aspect of the puker is evident in the moment of deepest denigration. What would you like? Could be butterflies?

Maybe hummingbirds would be a little more unusual. Or do you prefer plant life?

Why don't you care? This is a chance for self-expression, to show yourself as unbeatable in your essence. And that's an important message to get across to other incoming freshmen, not just the girls either because that would cause a lot of problems politically. You have no idea. So we're going to pitch this film to all genders.

So here's a question. So what's the residual pain like? Any aches and pains left over? We mean besides the termination of course. You feel it mostly in your legs? That's interesting. Because you fought a lot with your legs? Really? I'm not sure that makes sense. That's the point of the cocktail. No fighting. Girls are usually pretty compliant we hear, and then no memory. Oh, inside the window. Got it. That's when you were fighting. Well, that's really interesting. The cardplayers tried to come at you inside the store window. Like they were pretending they were in Amsterdam or something. That's pretty crazy. Where were these guys from? You don't know. We should just make them some kind of animal but surprising ones, not weasels or rats, like dolphins might be really ironic. What do you think?

Not much. Okay. You know, we just have to ask: Have you ever considered, hey, this window may all be your imagination? Some kind of hallucination? Or even, it happens, a kinky kind of fantasy? Okay. Okay. No, of course we believe you. That's why we're here. Okay. So you were kicking away the big gang in the store window.

But wait, why didn't you just fight them with your arms? That would be more typical. Your arms were still weak? The muscles wouldn't fire fast enough? Well, that must have been strange. So you kicked them? You were a champion swimmer in high school? Cool. That was lucky. Very lucky. So you kicked and then what? One guy goes right out through the glass window, boom, shattered. That must have been some cheap-ass old glass. It was already cracked? Makes sense. And you noticed that? It was like your brain was working and your eyes and your legs, but not your arms. That must have been weird.

How did you hold up your towel? You lost the towel, but eventually you took the sheet, okay. And the guys vanished when the window shattered, because an alarm went off inside the store. You got down on the floor and tried to wrap the sheet around you using your good feet because your hands kept losing the grip. By the time the police came you were like a bloody mummy, because the glass had cut you up. The mousetrap was stuck in your hair? We have to use that. And the police just drove you here? No questions asked? Wrapped in a sheet, covered in blood, with a mousetrap in your hair? Un-fucking-believable.

Right. Right. Right. The shooting. They needed to get over there fast. Honestly? We don't think that's an excuse. Which is why we're making this film. Did you know that this campus is in the top ten percentile of sexual assault in the whole country? Surprising, right? But it's in the bottom percentile of cases reported by the police. Well, that's our hook. That's why it's going to be big. That discrepancy.

So how long before you knew you were pregnant? Not that long. Okay. And did you need anything else, stitches, any emergency care? You decided against it. And how long until the feeling in your arms came back? Wow. That's a long time. Those cocktails are deadly. Truly. And what about now, any residual aches? Even just mentally?

Huh. Well, you look okay to us. I mean if we were going to do this live, and if it wasn't for the retaliatory nature of Reed and Peekskill, we would definitely use you because you have a lost look around your eyes that is kind of, no offense, awkward in person, big gaps in the flow of conversation. But on film it would be haunting and we could edit out the pauses, make a kind of staccato rhythm, as if you were edgy and fast thinking and on your feet, instead of staring and mystified. Definitely the message we want to send is one of empowerment. How to make good decisions in your life. How to be your own best advocate. How to look feminine, sure, but strong. Not someone who's going to put up with a lot of male intimidation and who can basically hold her liquor, even when drugged. Right? So a cartoon will definitely deliver that about you. We think we'd like to make you a starfish, but a pretty one.

Why? Because they can lose an essential part of themselves and then grow it right back. That's not true? Well, in cartoons it happens all the time. You've just got to believe us on that one.

All right. So. It's been like great talking to you. Thanks so much.

Looks like we've got everything we need.

No, more than enough.

No, plenty.

So, now the hard work begins. We've got to transpose all this to some sane and usable format. Figure and ground. Always the same question. Crazy, right? Technology thinks it's soaring beyond what's ever been known before to mankind while art stays perennial. Or something like that. What? Of course we'll stay in touch! Absolutely. We already feel like your best friends. This has been really great! Okay now. We're going. Aloha.

SUMMERSPACE

In the summer she would turn twenty-six, Cece worked as a part-time assistant in a temporary preschool in Brooklyn. Her boss, Lennie, grouchy Lennie, fox faced and thin, was experimenting with language at the Crestview Houses. These were a group of rusty dark mid-rises built in the forties near the Gowanus Canal. Lennie's experimental preschool operated out of the community room, which opened to a wedge of outdoor space with a swing set, a bench, and a few gingko trees. Junipers sprawled low in oval-shape beds. Sometimes Cece liked to sit there under the trees and draw after school. One of the children would join her or at least circle around.

Usually Lennie left school immediately, locking the community room behind her. On her way past Cece, a quick flat-handed salute, a reminder of warnings already issued. Then she'd rush off to tabulate the day's observations while still fresh. She had the taut, expectant mouth of a secret smoker. Her hair was buzzed and bleached.

Cece's hair was something she was ignoring, yanked tight into a ponytail and forgotten. This emphasized a wide-eyed quality Lennie felt they could all live without. Cece's shoulders curled forward around her drawing pad. She had a goofy unconscious smile when she drew. Lennie was photo shy. Cece was not. Cece's mother, Faith, liked to say that Cece's face hadn't altered since the day she was born. An observation, if she knew, Lennie could have believed.

Now the summer was just about over, and Lennie's preschool was closing at the Crestview Houses. For the autumn, she had a better opportunity in the Bronx. Tomorrow Cece's best-ever paycheck would be suspended.

As Cece saw it, her main duties at Lennie's preschool had been to keep the kids from running away from all the enrichment, running straight up to the edge of the stillborn canal and jumping in. Overjoyed, as if those half-submerged steel prongs were inflatable toys.

But she still had the English bulldogs to walk on Pacific Street. And a colicky baby boy terrorizing his parents on Baltic. Any time Cece could give them was gratefully received. She was also a "researcher" for Mrs. O'Hara, the retired Macy's dress buyer working on an imaginary history of her ancestors. Mrs. O'Hara lived housebound on Atlantic Avenue. Her current focus: a mysterious great-great-grandmother, very possibly a Gallatin. A gifted botanist who'd ruined her career by murdering the nanny. She'd been hanged! Which was the heart of Mrs. O'Hara's mystery. Hanged? When streets and towns were named for her? Cece's job was to make strong oolong tea and take notes on any new discoveries. Then, according to Mrs. O'Hara's instructions, Cece typed up scenes. Scenes of intense ardor. Even the nanny's murder was only a moment of confused devotion.

Most of her employers appreciated Cece's gentleness. They all used the word. But Lennie deemed this quality a liability at the Crestview Houses. Cece's summer evaluation had been waiting in an envelope on the snack table this very afternoon. *Cece certainly loves the children, but we're doubtful about the academic quality of her input.*

That was it. Two copies. One to be signed and returned to Lennie the next day. And then Cece would take a slow train for a nonnegotiable visit to her mother on the Jersey Shore.

Which was lousy timing because just last night, a text had arrived from her old friend Sebastian. He was in Brooklyn! Not Nepal, not Kashmir. Actually in Carroll Gardens with his sister, Chloe, and her new baby, Karl Jr. Sebastian had sent a photo of a gluey-looking infant in close-up. Eyes matted and miserable. A widemouthed cry of alarm. Cece understood. Again and again, Sebastian was being prompted to spontaneous joy or else. And just twenty-four hours in, his well of delight had run dry. Cece looked at the baby midwail and smiled. Save me, Sebastian texted. He begged to stay at her place for just a day or two. Save me. Cece's place was a dark studio on the street level. His admiration muscles could relax there.

Yes. Yes. Meet me after work, four o'clock, she replied. She sent a map to the Crestview Houses, to the swing-set area outside the community room. About a ten-minute walk from his sister's home.

But in her experience, Sebastian often got lost on the way to anywhere. It amazed her to think of him in Nepal. He was on the creative team with a Danish NGO working on inflatable housing? Disposable housing? Anyway, something flat-packed and easily erected in extremity. Political unrest. Disastrous weather. All this she knew from a long email he'd sent in February. Also Sebastian's general wish to see her. To say something a bit overdue, okay? Before that, it had been years without a word.

Lately, Cece was toying with the idea of another class at Hunter College. In the spring, she'd taken Shakespeare, the comedies. Over the summer, she'd audited a broad-stroke English survey course. A grab bag—Wordsworth, Dickinson, Morrison, Burroughs.

If only Cece would buckle down and take actual courses for credit, her mother said. By December she could complete her freshman year! Faith also said Cece's life was her own to ruin now.

Even so, Faith had hoped—demanded, really—that Cece spend this last summer weekend on the shore. Together they'd close up her grandmother's house in Spring Lake. Leased out as a seasonal rental now that her grandmother was gone. Faith and Cece would sweep away all the summer strangers. Repair the beloved garden. This isn't optional, said Faith.

Someday soon, her mother and uncle would need to put her grandmother's house up for sale, but for now, her mother had agreed, *temporarily* the summer rental income in Spring Lake could subsidize Cece's sublet in Brooklyn, as long as she pitched in on the cleanup. A disheartening arrangement for Cece. But not one she could refuse. So she'd named a train time and she couldn't change now without serious complaint from Faith. But tonight! Sebastian! Here, in Brooklyn. She'd give him a key. He could stay as long as he liked.

Well past four o'clock and only Cece and her preschool student Clarence were outside now at the Crestview Houses. Cece had spread sheets of drawing paper on the sodden bench under the gingko trees. Clarence lay belly down on one of the new hard plastic swings. These had replaced the sling-style eco-friendly seats that Lennie had sourced and installed in June. The eco-swings were immediately deemed unacceptable by the community. Slashed to shreds in the night by bored teenagers. The replacement swings were hard and backward looking, maybe, but bladeproof. They were also heavy. Clarence dragged his sneakers in the mud and never achieved liftoff. This was a soothing activity Cece understood. She would not exhort him to sit up and pump even during school hours. And besides he was only keeping an eye on her, until the guy arrived. Whoever he was.

Cece was a source of fascination among the preschoolers at Crestview. She was so often in trouble with the boss, Lennie, so often in the wrong. And even after a sudden heavy August downpour—with hail!—sent everyone inside to escape the wet, noxious steam that followed, a scout was required, Clarence, to watch and see just what kind of craziness would show up for Cece today.

Cece sat cross-legged on the bench and waited. She was thinking about whether to discuss her work evaluation with Sebastian. She thought of him as strategic or maybe just opportunistic, and that could be a blank spot for her. Clarence was sticking out his tongue to indicate boredom.

Chess, Clarence?

Clarence took his time answering. This was too sweet an offer. To be held in suspicion until other factors clarified his decision. Like the imagined approval or disapproval of his friends. Cece was someone to be toyed with, sure, but to be placated sometimes, too, all at a very low level, so not to mess her up. Her volatility was something they'd never seen. Or rather its clamped-down expression. Like she'd swallowed a burning helicopter but didn't know it. So they were careful with her, and she didn't know that either.

Clarence was already five years old and in the fall he'd be in kindergarten on the older end of his class, but in the track for kids unlikely to read well, ever. Lennie offered all kinds of language-enrichment modules at her experimental preschool, but Clarence was indifferent, and this indifference had influenced his public school placement. The only kid, as far as Cece knew, to get such a low recommendation.

This outcome, this *lifetime* prediction about Clarence, based solely on Lennie's fleeting opinion made Cece want to burst into tears, and she did know that much. The fury she felt at her employer. Just thinking about it. The burst of spikey rage. *Lennie should be arrested!* And the odd contrasting peace sitting on this wet bench, under the dripping trees, a brief hop from the superfund canal that glugged through the neighborhood, the little boy, whose rude pink tongue on lazy display was meant to insult her but calmed her instead. Come on, Clarence, she said. Play some chess.

Cece's version of chess wasn't the one that Clarence's sister, Deirdre, loaded on her phone to distract him. Cece's chess had to do with a thick drawing pad she kept in her backpack. That and some worn-down crayons. She would draw something; Clarence would draw something. It was boring until it wasn't. She'd study the shapeless blobs he made on purpose. It wasn't like he would show her anything. But she got so interested it seemed like he was winning, so he did end up drawing stuff.

Inside the community room, the official crayons were in primary colors only. But now the crayons and paper and Legos and whiteboards and plush floor cushions shaped like frogs and beavers were already packed away in Thule crates. Lennie had posted notices around Crestview Houses about her move to the Bronx for new data in the fall. Goodbye.

Clarence's sister, Deirdre, said, No big loss. But Clarence wasn't so sure. What about the music? He didn't say. That had been nice. And what about Jokes 101? That had been Cece's big idea. Who cares, said Deirdre. You're done with that now.

No one would come outside soon, so Clarence slid off the swing in slow motion and walked sideways. He could change his mind if anyone opened a window and shouted out a different guidance from above. But the loudest thing was the air conditioners choking for coolness inside. No one would come out into this. So he made it all the way to Cece's bench, where she'd started drawing without him. Cheater!

He picked up a crayon in his fist. A reject color, something mauve. Cece only carried the odd ones.

I'll start over, she said. Not looking at him, she flipped to a fresh page. Immediately she drew an angular crushed-looking flower. Clarence began to correct what a flower usually did on his side of the page. So far the mauve would work out.

Tomorrow, for the final day, there wasn't much on the schedule. The kids could officially say goodbye and pick up a certificate. There would be juice. But Deirdre didn't see the point of Clarence going. You're finished with that bullshit, okay?

It looked like Cece might be finished with that bullshit, too. As she colored in some fronds, she realized she didn't need cunning Sebastian to tell her she wouldn't be invited to the Bronx. Because Lennie knew, and Cece knew herself, that she wasn't likely to ever *really* be an educator, experimental or otherwise. And she wouldn't be reinventing the language of crisis housing like Sebastian either. And no doctoral program for Cece, like the one awaiting her amateur therapist, Kai McCann—quite suddenly her former therapist. Kai would go to Columbia in January after tidying up her thesis in the fall. And Cece would continue to slow-walk bulldogs, type up love-saturated murders for Mrs. O'Hara, calm the deepest fret of a baby boy.

*　*　*

During Cece's Shakespeare semester at Hunter College, a free student mental health counseling service, a pop-up, was offered. Colloquially—and experientially, in Cece's view—called the amateurs. Clinical social work students doing a little service research. In February, actually not long after Sebastian's surprise email arrived from Nepal, Cece had filled out a form. What the hell, it was only one page. All about childhood, ages zero to twenty-one. Ten one-word questions: Divorce? Desertion? Death? Illness? Addiction? And so on. Each question had an additional line to fill in only if the box had been checked. Who went to prison? And that was it. She was told she'd be notified by text if her questionnaire found an interested counselor in training. She also signed a disclaimer about what little help to actually expect. But she was curious.

Late May, to her surprise, Cece had been chosen. The grad students set up shop for the summer in an old gym. Her new counselor, Kai McCann, was at least a year or two younger than Cece, with a baby face she offset with a black wedge of hair on one side, shaved irritated stubble on the other. Kai wore a uniform for her research, blue oxford-cloth button-downs, emphatically wrinkled. The weekly sessions in the gym began in early June. By August, Cece had come to appreciate Kai, her irascible, unsuitable nature, the sweat-saturated stink of the consulting cubicle. Therapy with Kai was like playing house with the least friendly kid in the neighborhood.

* * *

It was so hot now at the Crestview Houses the rocks under the juniper bushes let off a greenish steam. Clarence was deciding if his leaves needed some extra points on the sides—probably yes—when he saw a shadow slither along the ground. Cece was concentrating on the mashed-up tree she was coloring, wrongly, in burnt orange, so she missed it entirely, but Clarence let his eyes slide over toward the nearest door.

Cece dotted grooves on her tree trunk before glancing up, too. Nothing. Just a wind gust shaking the branches. They both went back to drawing but tentatively, because there were hard rules about Cece's presence here. Mostly to do with light and time. But also equipment. In daylight, before five in the afternoon—but not after, no matter how bright the sun—and as long as she had something educational in her hand, like the drawing pad, she was welcome here.

Welcome was too strong a word. Lennie had talked to Cece about her blindness, her naivete, her stupefying tra-la-la worldview. This pep talk had come after the teenage boys who'd slashed the sling-style eco-swings had cornered Cece late one afternoon in June on the bench under the gingko trees where she was sitting now.

They were big boys, thirteen, twelve. And they knew how to intimidate. They practiced on each other. That's really all they were doing here: practicing, playing, surrounding this dopey young woman staring off into space. Didn't she have a home of her own to stare and be foolish in? They just asked her for their old swings back. Quietly. The splintery wooden ones that had been replaced by useless sling-style trash. At least that's how it started.

They were tall now and that was only recent and they were still finding out how that might work. On the subway, for instance, if they leaned close to each other around a seated woman, kind of encased her with their new tall bodies and said some loud very explicit things, over the lady's head, about the girls they were fucking or would be soon, that usually got at least a frown. So it was really only that. A choreography they were still playing around with that had them draw in close to Cece, sitting too late on a sunny afternoon in June, and muse, just to each other, out loud, what the fuck had happened to the old swings? They liked the old swings just fine. But something seemed to happen to Cece that was new to them. They were just kidding around, but she was melting, like they were made of fire. Her face was getting strange, and it scared them.

When Cece was still in regular college—it seemed a long time ago but only five years, almost six years really—on the glorious campus with the mountain sunsets and the woodland paths, back when she was a regular freshman, the very worst thing hadn't been the attack itself or the gawkers and the filmmakers who came later but Sebastian's near-immediate withdrawal from what had been the sweetest friendship of her life. As if she'd survived something life extinguishing only to be felled by a snub.

But she hadn't known it was possible to find a friend that tender, that funny. Oh, sweetheart, her mother had said. That's college for you.

But her mother had no idea about real college. And now neither would Cece, ever. In a moment of desperation, she'd told Faith all about losing Sebastian. She'd told her nothing else and probably never would. But just before Cece left school for good, she called her mother and told her how, on a dime, he stopped being her friend. She was sobbing by the end.

Oh, honey! Faith had sounded so helpless. Sweetheart, sweetheart. I'm coming. As if Cece were a fussy infant in the next room. Then: Cece, my love, you do know it couldn't possibly be about you. His mother is so—

This isn't about his mother! Cece cried.

Okay, said Faith. Okay. Well, then. I wonder if for you, this friendship was maybe—

Oh no, said Cece.

I'm just wondering—

He really doesn't, Mom, said Cece, angry now. He doesn't.

Well, he reminded *me* of your brother, said Faith. Something in his walk? When I first met him.

This was the trouble with Faith. Virtually everyone reminded her of Cece's little brother. He had died when they were tiny. A freak accident and he was gone, except for Faith, who saw her son everywhere. Cece didn't have the heart to tell Faith she had no memory of that time. Cece couldn't tell Faith because it would leave her mother all alone with her unquenchable loss.

That night on the phone, she managed to croak out a pinched reversal: Possibly? Possibly you're right. And then a goodbye, because if she didn't Faith would call her back immediately.

Maybe it was a week later, maybe two, but college stopped making sense soon after that call.

Recently, her mental health counselor, Kai McCann, had something interesting to say to Cece. She'd probably read the material on her phone that morning. But she told Cece something she didn't already know. After an assault, Kai began. It was strange to hear that word, but Kai used it a lot. It was discordant, like a mismatch for what Cece remembered or mostly didn't remember. It seemed too specific and large. But Cece had checked the box for sexual assault on the form, and she'd told Kai about it during their first session, as if with Kai, who so clearly didn't know what she was doing, it didn't really count. So Kai said attack, assault, rape, and she said it often.

After an assault, Kai said, he, they, whoever, might send, I don't know what you want to call them, rovers? Anyway, the rapist sends people to mill around. To make a larger point. There needs to be a community to really be effective. Schools, obviously. Churches. In random rape, this doesn't happen. But think about helicopters that soar around a neighborhood for no reason but sound menacing. They never land. They never actually do anything. You know, rovers? Kai

McCann smoothed the wrinkled collar on the button-down, then scratched her forehead, methodically, just above each eyebrow.

So many little tics to sort out before Kai was even a little bit good at this. Still, Cece nodded. The rovers?

Yes. Kai thought that might be why the Crestview boys had felt so problematic. Remember?

But that wasn't what happened at Crestview. The tall boys were only playing. Just learning how to be themselves. Wasn't that the whole point of the experimental preschool, amplification of inherent strength? What was so different about these boys balancing on their toes to catch an extra inch? And holding still, because that was sometimes better. They'd figured that out already. Hold still. Stand really straight. Keep your eyes open. Don't all talk at once. Create a little pattern. Overlap, yes. But not chaos. They were still working things out, and Cece understood that, listening to them, looking up at them—and she knew they were right about the eco-swings, which would have disintegrated in a year's time—but then something else happened. Despite everything she understood about these very young men—boys—she was coming apart. She felt terrified and they felt it, too. And it confused them about themselves. And the confusion made them angry. What about our fucking swings?

*   *   *

Beginning that summer, Clarence on Thursdays in the late afternoon had to go to Key Food with Deirdre to help carry home the groceries. Get used to it, she said. But she gave him the light sacks to carry, and when they dragged on the sidewalk, she would stop and reload.

As usual, close to home, something got too heavy, so they paused on the corner, and right at that moment Clarence looked up. Over on the bench, Cece was crying. That was a bad idea.

Don't think I'm carrying those for you, said Deirdre. Clarence, you hear me? What's the matter with you? But then she looked where he was looking and saw the problem. Can you believe how stupid?

It was certainly stupid to cry in front of the big boys.

Deirdre stretched all the way over then and clutched her knees, as if her back was killing her. Clarence had seen this movement again and again, usually on his mother and now on Deirdre. It made her look like an old lady, but she was only fifteen so far. Tell that dumb girl I sprained my ankle.

Clarence looked at his sister. You did?

You heard me. Run. Go.

Clarence ran. Deirdre sprained her ankle! Deirdre sprained her ankle! He sang out over and over like a game. Deirdre sprained her ankle! He swung his arms around for emphasis. Deirdre! Deirdre sprained her ankle!

He reeled up to the gathering around the bench and paused. Through the stockade of boys' arms, Cece's face was extra white and frozen now. But tears were still coming, like someone else in her body had taken over the crying.

173

Clarence spiraled his arms again, just slightly, and said, Deirdre?

What's that?

Now the boys looked around at him. It was possible they would have a different idea about the sprained ankle, the groceries, the crying girl who sometimes drew interesting things on her pad. There could be a whole new interpretation coming, and Clarence waited.

What are you shouting about?

Clarence rarely had this much attention all at once, except when Lennie stared him down in the language-acquisition modules, and once again ideas seemed to stop in his head. What had he just been saying?

You're the bug we squashed yesterday. Back again? Now the boys were all turning and staring at him. Instead of standing on their tiptoes, they were squatting down, testing out the power of physical closeness on a lower level. Clarence remembered something. Words are little pictures, that's all. No big deal. Cece had wedged that into his stopped brain when Lennie gave up and moved on to the more promising kids. Pictures? he'd said. Cece had nodded. He got that. That was pretty obvious.

Deirdre sprained her ankle! Deirdre sprained her ankle. Her ankle is shot. Shot! Her back is one big fat ugly mess of pain.

One big ugly mess of pain was something the boys had all heard before. A more familiar confusion began sifting in. The old confusion all the new choreography was meant to solve.

You shitheads get over here and pick up these groceries!
Now! Deirdre shouted.

This was an order they couldn't possibly follow. They
couldn't even indicate they'd heard it. But one could peel off
and laugh about what Deirdre had going on with her grocery
bags spread out all over the sidewalk like garbage. And another could go over and register fresh disgust about the new
swings. The idea of a mess of pain reminded another boy his
mother had asked him to do something he'd forgotten. And
so they dispersed. Clarence ambled off to the swings, too,
bad as they were. And Deirdre rearranged the grocery sacks
so she could carry them home.

So, what about the rovers? The people who milled around her
on campus? The ones who studied her like an art project?

Right! And when did they finally disperse? Kai asked
Cece.

Disperse?

Right. When did they stop?

The answer of course was never, and Kai McCann knew
that.

The sky began to darken again right above the canal, as if the
sludge had been used to color in the clouds. Ominous. Clarence glanced up at the sky then went back to his drawing. He
was sketching long curling lines, strings or wires, attached

to the points on the leaves. Cece was coloring in pink grass around her burnt-orange tree. She wasn't much of an artist, but she liked artists. In school, she'd always been drawn to them. Even now, Lennie and her arty slant on preschool had been a draw. Above all, Sebastian had seemed radiant to her. The first thing she'd noticed besides his slender height and his rubber-tire earring, was the black wire dangling from beneath his T-shirt. And it had stopped her breath. She remembered this even now. Not being able to find her breath. This boy goofing on their prefab dormitories had wire dangling, which meant, of course, a medical device of some kind. Sebastian, in the greenish lighting saw her face twitch and right away lifted his shirt and she gasped. He had electrodes, three of them, attached to key parts of his chest. The wires tangled and gathered in a black pouch on his belt loop. Sebastian grinned, then he dropped his shirt without explaining.

A few days later the wires no longer dangled. The pouch was gone. But she was alert to his presence by then, and that alertness was the beginning of something. For most of her only semester, he would seek her out and show her things. Drawings. Poems. Pocket sculptures in white flaky plaster. And each time he waited for her face to go through its changes. He relied on her. Like a blood test.

Did she love Sebastian? She thought she did. She thought they loved each other. Even later when she heard the wires were a joke, a project. Equipment his mother had needed to monitor a chemotherapy and its wayward impact on her heart. Sebastian had worn the discard as an experiment, for fun. It was the one project she thought she really understood. He missed his mother, just as she missed hers. A big surprise, this longing for Faith. Cece had been eager, frantic even to get away from home. But she ached for her impossible mother. Then Sebastian appeared. The balm. The tender focus. Life's recalibrator. And then he vanished, gone. Kai, the amateur therapist, wanted to zero in on that departure.

This week, when Cece showed up at Kai McCann's cubicle for their appointment, Kai had arranged some yellow Post-it squares in a half circle on the partition wall. Most had stick figures notable for their erect balloon-shape penises. The center Post-it had the two stick guys with the biggest balloons. RAPISTS, Kai had printed in, helpfully, in block letters.

On another square, many guys crowded together— maybe four, no, five. The rovers? said Cece.

Kai nodded.

Then there was a single stick guy, alone, his yellow square at an angle. Unlike the others, his balloon penis pointed downward to one side, as if about to be fitted for an expensive pair of trousers. This was all incredibly odd. Early on, Cece had told Kai that she liked to draw with the kids at Crestview. Clearly a sickening mistake. On the desk, more pads and Sharpies at the ready.

Interesting, right? said Kai. She made her semi-ironic we're-in-this-together grimace. Cece had learned all of Kai's expressions over the summer.

No stick figure for me? said Cece.

That's good, said Kai. She made a fast-typed note on her phone. Or maybe just sent a text.

Cece took the visitor chair and shook her head. Really, Kai, this is— But then she started to laugh.

Come on. Just try it. Kai pointed her Sharpie to the stand-alone. For instance, who's this guy?

The one with the downward balloon?

Right. What does that say?

Well, said Cece. He's a bystander? And not so interested?

Okay. What's he doing?

Nothing?

Nothing? Really?

Cece sighed. It was a ragged sigh.

Is he someone you know? Kai said.

Maybe not?

Listen, said Kai, leaning forward with sudden clarity. We're exploring the roles you're assigning. Maybe you're putting people on the wrong Post-it? Or just adding the wrong labels.

Cece felt herself blush. She was embarrassed for Kai but didn't know how to steer things in a better direction. I don't know, Kai, isn't this—she made the you-and-me hand gesture Kai usually liked—supposed to be more evocative?

Evocative. Kai wrote it down on a new Post-it.

It's like you've prearranged the story and yet I'm still being quizzed. It's very strange.

Quizzed. Kai scratched vigorously at the stubble side of her head. Sure, I see that.

You do?

Sure, said Kai. And I'm kind of struck by something.

Oh?

You remember that oral exam I had to take.

Cece shook her head.

Anyway, it was insanely hard. Like an inquisition. And I'd had no sleep for days. I don't even know if I was talking in complete syllables. I think it may have imprinted me.

Okay.

But I passed. Don't worry.

Cece tried to refocus on the Post-its, then she looked back at Kai. Congratulations?

You can add some squares, too, if you feel like it, said Kai. Look, like this. She stood and pasted EVOCATIVE near the others. Then she sat and glanced down at her phone. Oh my god. Are we really out of time? Were you late?

I don't think so.

I didn't notice. Anyway, we have to stop and talk about the fall.

The fall?

Sure. Because Kai thought, you know, given everything, they might leave the counseling up in the air for now. Cece was doing amazingly well. And maybe Kai should just jam ahead on her master's thesis and be done with it. What did Cece think?

Cece studied Kai's face across the desk for a long time. As if this were actual therapy and she were actually thinking. She'd never felt it appropriate to ask. But she asked now:

179

What's your thesis topic, Kai? Cece waved at the stick figures. Something about sexual assault? I'd guess that's pretty popular right now.

Well, no. It's a little more off the main drag.

Uh-huh.

Yes, it's the impact of a sibling's death on children. On the surviving siblings.

What?

Yeah, you know, said Kai. She let a slack fingertip point toward Cece.

You mean *me?*

Yes. Of course.

But? But you never asked me a single thing about that.

Well, I'm more interested in what's happening now. *So much* about the parents. Almost zero on the kids, especially grown-up.

I don't understand, Kai. I really don't remember anything.

Right! I know! Which is fascinating.

Cece felt her eyes squint nearly shut involuntarily, like a loud light had been shoved at her. Not bright, *loud.* It made no sense.

You're perfect for me, said Kai. She offered one of her favorite therapeutic gestures, an appreciative head nod with soft closed-mouth smile.

This was far beyond Kai's usual ineptness. Something like disgust billowed up in Cece's throat. A feeling almost unknown to her.

Okay. Kai pushed back in her chair. So, anyway.

But Cece kept very still. Finally she picked up a Sharpie and a pad. She stared at Kai as if for a portrait.

I get it, said Kai. I get it. Recruiting a friend! Very good! But they're actually going to lock up the gym. Some kind of weird half holiday. Who knows. Anyway, I think we're probably finished here, don't you? It's been amazing getting to know you.

Cece bent over the table and carefully drew a stick figure with a bubble head. Shaved stubble dots on one side and a black wedge on the other, a button-down shirt. Stick legs. Big boots.

She stood up to study the half circle on the wall and then realized she needed to add some identifying block letters. She worked them in. Then she pressed the Kai figure right on top of the bystander Post-it. It was hard to read because the letters were so squished, but it said: STRANGER. And also, politely: GOODBYE.

Then Cece zigzagged out through the haphazard cubicles and pushed hard on the swinging gym doors. Wait! she heard Kai shout behind her. Wait, you've got me all wrong!

But Kai was right. Therapy was finished now for Cece. And her mother, Faith, was correct, too. Cece wouldn't be moving closer to any kind of useful degree. And she might not go on a date, either. Though nobody had offered an opinion on that front. She wasn't against a profession or love. More like the impulse or intrigue or curiosity or drive or desire had tipped over and stopped without her noticing.

But she would like to take another English course. Lately, Cece was interested in Dorothy Wordsworth. She'd popped up as a side note in the summer survey class. Her lifelong devotion to her brother, the poet. Her exquisite lists. Words without context or meaning. As if *he* were her only context. *He* was the only meaning. That couldn't possibly be true. That couldn't be the whole story.

Five o'clock and still no sign of Sebastian. She'd already re-sent the map. But only once. The bells of St. Agnes began their loud raucous exuberance. You never knew what song the bells might play now that they were computerized. Often old show tunes—"Hello Dolly"?—rarely a hymn.

The closest entrance to the Crestview Houses was a wide metal door painted a lemony green topped with a striped metal awning at the end of a winding walk. The awning, the twisty walk, the junipers in oval beds nodded to a fierce negotiation long ago about what was absolutely necessary for postwar urban housing. For all the returning soldiers who'd need a new kind of home.

Now the bright metal door squealed open, as if rigged for this very alert. Both Clarence and Cece looked up. But it was just Deirdre. She stood under the awning surveying the scene with displeasure. Deirdre was a short, compact girl with an abundance of long braided hair, today tucked under a blue cap. Like Clarence, she was dark skinned. Her shorts and top were new. Clarence and Cece looked back at their drawings.

Deirdre took her time on the winding path, looking around, as if scouting for storm damage, but the hail, so dramatic, had already dissolved. Everything was just steamy and for the moment smelled of soapy fabric. A vent from the laundromat across the street had briefly doused the air.

Are you behaving? Deirdre called out to Clarence.

Yes, he said. The right answer to a frequent question. It allowed Deirdre to come closer.

Are you sitting on wet?

No, said Cece, smiling up at Deirdre. I wiped things off.

I hear you're getting fired.

Maybe. Probably not renewed.

Yeah, well. I already told him it's no big deal. Okay? This thing wasn't much, you know? Come on, bug. We're going to Key Food now.

Cece began packing up the crayons and the pad while Clarence stood up to go, as usual, as if he'd see her tomorrow afternoon, just as before.

He's not a big talker, Deirdre said.

Cece nodded. She understood. It was a disappointing outcome for Clarence. All this enrichment, and nothing would be any better for him. Quite possibly worse. Cece was disappointed, too. Though now that she thought about it, she might go over to his new school. She knew exactly which one. She would ask to speak with his teacher. There were things she could say. Why not try?

Cece looked to Clarence, then at the pad in her hands. She flipped open to the pages they'd been working on together.

She touched the point on one of Clarence's flowers. This is very nice, she said, widening her eyes, because it was. And Clarence gave the kind of grin Cece loved, on anyone really, a glimpse of the person newborn to old, all at once.

He doesn't talk a lot, but he talks about *you*. Deirdre was lodging a different complaint now. He talks about all this shit. Deirdre waved at the pad and crayons. He says he's just trying to teach you something. But you're not that smart.

Cece looked into Deirdre's determined, curious, never-miss-a-trick eyes and saw where Clarence might be going next, if he was lucky.

True, Cece said, as if saying something she could only just begin to know.

Yeah. Well. Don't forget. Whatever it was.

FRAGILE X

1.

Faith hadn't been to the Beach Club in years and years. I wouldn't know a soul anymore, she said, nervous, wooing a potential new client. Her bookkeeping, business-planning venture had formed slowly, mistake by mistake. But by now she thought she knew what she was doing. Right away, Faith had mentioned her daughter Cece's looming visit. Children, always the first subject. Disarming, Faith had learned.

And the potential client, Jill Marks, looked as if Faith had just delighted her. She'd only said that Cece, like Jill's young daughter, had been a swimmer. The 6:00 a.m. swim team practices, the green Speedos, and the freezing water in the saltwater pool, splashing her feet, while she stood, dutifully, drinking tepid coffee from a paper cup. This was after Bernadette left and of course after the brief and bitter rule of Lee-Ann. Then she'd taken Cece to the club herself. In all the summers that followed, she'd taken Cece. So she could swim.

Wait, said Jill Marks. Tell me where your cabana was.

The club was always terrible in this way. Bald in its rank-
ing of members. Oh, said Faith, waving it off. I forget. Maybe
third from the end?

You mean the stand-alones?

I don't think we called them that, laughed Faith. More
like the huts. They were a disaster, leaky roofs, impossible
bathrooms. Rust. Rust as design element! And then she felt
they'd done enough preliminary talk. She pulled a yellow
legal pad out of a tote bag, pushed forward the lead on a mechanical pencil. This wasn't just a signal to the client. Since
starting her business, Faith had learned how much these
gestures helped her.

But Jill Marks was still smiling as if they were old friends,
reconnecting, reconstructing the lost years.

Oh, they don't bother with the coffee anymore, Jill said.
Green juice! There we all are: the green suits, the juice, the awn-
ings, green everything! Honestly, they could use your help.

Faith smiled but unsteadily. Her help?

Well, said Jill Marks with a wave toward the blue enamel
of the Italian espresso machine. The lofty new windows of
the coffee shop. As if Faith's presence here were enough to
make things very nice indeed.

Faith sighed audibly, and Jill finally slipped a large cell
phone out of a pink leather sleeve. Okay, she said. Here's
the thing.

It was almost a good idea. Jill was creating a babysitting
service slash rehabilitation job training. Kids who needed a
second chance but not much of one. These were teenagers

who'd gotten into a little bit of trouble, suspended from school for tardiness or in a fender bender with a questionable friend at the wheel and so on.

Now Faith held back the sigh and found she was also holding her breath—heard her mother say, What's the trouble, bubble? Nothing, she hoped. And Jill Marks talked on and on. She spoke of the young miscreants like adorable merchandise that would fly off the shelves. It was very odd to Faith but not unfamiliar. Children as units to be shifted. After all, how had she landed here in the chic coffee shop? Courtney Ruddy. Who even now liked to keep a hand in.

Ten years ago—at least, more—Courtney had left J. P. Morgan and the Jersey Shore to marry, for the first time, a much older poet living in Upstate New York. The shock! Faith attended the wedding out of pure curiosity. She found a cluster of swaying, graying men, mostly, on a steep hillside overlooking a cow pond. They recited many poems. Faith remembers the way her legs felt—on fire—high heels sinking into the loose soil. And the way Courtney looked nymph-like and beautiful, like a sexy child, in the company of these men. Just this week she'd written to say she'd tossed Faith's number to a young entrepreneur. She needs a bookkeeper and a bit of good sense. Don't thank me!

2.

Hadley's eyes felt as if they'd been poked hard by small sandy fingers while he slept. A dense pinching throb. Here come the jasmine towels delivered on a tray. A scent he disliked, but the damp and heat might help. Also a handful of aspirin and a last-minute vodka. Then the gray Atlantic below would give way to the suburban beaches of Long Island. The usual tangle at Kennedy Airport awaited. Boris would be there, as always, leaning against the wall with the other drivers. The town car parked someplace close and illegal. Boris waving like family as Hadley emerged into the International Arrivals area. Before that, a shuffle and slide through customs. It would be tedious and fine. Then he'd be in the car heading home. A bike courier could take Owen's dubious gift the rest of the way downtown.

Delayed, apparently, the plane began coasting in the wider, slower circles. They dipped down over the flame-shooting oil refineries of Elizabeth. On the Jersey Turnpike, cars moved faster than the plane tilted in a mid-air stall. He hated being a messenger for his brother. It makes me a liar, he thought, like a kid. Like they were still boys and Owen had a new bad plan. Something they'd be whipped for later. He could almost smile. And any number of people would smile along with him at the idea of Hadley taking umbrage at a lie. But he'd agreed. It's nothing! Owen had said in Hong Kong. Now the nothing was stuffed into a sparkly pink suitcase and stowed at the front of the cabin.

Finally, they landed. Immediately, there was a problem. A burst of new construction had erupted while he was away. The flight from Paris roamed lost around the runways for an hour.

Off the plane, at last, he carried little with him. Just a briefcase and small leather grip. What they might want to look for—but, really, why would they?—had already been walked through customs by the flight attendant. Hadley fixed his eyes on the sliding glass doors beyond the makeshift stations and put something tired and fond into his face, as if a wife, a daughter were waiting. The new customs area was only half-built so far. A temporary setup of folding vinyl-top tables and clamp lights on trellises, while the more formidable black booths were still underway. The trick was to stroll right through.

Over here, sir, waved an official. Right here, please.

Hadley looked ahead through the glass doors to his imaginary wife and saw Boris, his driver, bobbing in the crowd.

Right here. Passport, please.

Hadley puffed air through his lips, the weary traveler, and pulled the passport from his blazer pocket.

The agent thumbed to the most recent visa, then more slowly, after a glance up, he turned the pages backward one at a time. He got to the photograph, the address. Closed the passport, kept it curled in his hand, signaled a supervisor with a cough. Please follow me, he said.

Hadley turned to look at Boris once more, face drained. Now, sir.

When he saw Boris go still, he nodded to the officer and reached for his bag and briefcase.

Don't touch those. Come with me.

A second official was already diverting passengers to other tables or out the sliding glass doors. Yet another man in sweatpants with a badge clipped to a sun visor stepped forward to photograph Hadley's grip and briefcase from several angles with a square black camera.

Right now, sir.

I don't understand. What are you doing?

The official stepped closer to Hadley. He had deep crescents of red under his eyes, like someone with an allergy or a tragedy. He said in a low voice: I don't want to touch you.

All right, said Hadley, and he didn't look for Boris again.

They went out a pair of swinging rubberized doors through an unlit vestibule stacked with lost luggage, then into a bright hallway. The official knocked before opening a door. They were in an empty foyer now, just old blue plastic chairs pushed against new sheetrock. Then they were in a second room with a table, a telephone, and a plate glass window looking out to equipment parked under a steel canopy. The room had a din, the concentrated sound of several engines running at once. Take a seat, said the official. Then he stepped out, closed the door, and flipped the bolt lock.

3.

Jill Marks clicked open a file on her phone to show Faith the proposed floor plan of a space. The training center. A loft above the old furniture store right next to the hospital. And then, incongruently, a list of the speakers Jill would like to invite to visit. Political. High profile. She seemed to believe that sleepy suburban childcare and urban social justice formed an essential chemistry.

And maybe she was right. Faith would be the last to claim insight here. Cece, when she spoke to Faith at all, liked to walk her through the vectors of atrocity. She used the phrase without irony. The atrocities often referred to the deep confusing pockets of sorrow Cece had learned about in graduate school—graduate school!—Cece had learned to clear and organize confusion for other suffering children. It was always other children or teens, always young people. But Faith understood. She understood that in Cece's mind one thing (Cece's childhood) had led to a terrible other. And that's why, for years, she'd told Faith nothing. And when she did, she couldn't bear to listen to even one word from Faith about the "incident." Faith must keep her horror and rage, her reeling sadness, all of it, to herself. But Cece did talk about the textbook cases. Then cases in the clinic. Then finally her own clients, only just recently. The tiniest patients, a handful to start. Cece was still under supervision.

With bright happy eyes—so unlike her tender searching Cece, and Faith now realized they were about the same age—Jill Marks said she would sketch one sample miscreant up for renewal at her center. Just as an illustration. So Faith could get a feel for the goals. A fifteen-year-old girl with a bit of a craving for violent romantic adventure. Jill said she wouldn't go into specifics. But then came a long vivid description of this girl's pierced and scarified labia. And some speculation, in lurid detail, of where those expressive labia might have landed her recently. Jill Marks winced. Then added a world-savvy smile. This young woman with the loose chignon, the Hermès ready-to-wear. Her fifth-month belly decoratively buckled and zipped.

Faith stared at Jill Marks in disbelief. Then she felt herself go rigid. Even from Upstate New York, Courtney Ruddy had delivered her bull's-eye.

4.

Hadley picked up the phone. An old analog with push buttons on the dead receiver. Naturally his mobile was in his briefcase. He followed a tangled line to the wall jack, then the door squealed like a hinge being forced with a screwdriver. Someone taller now, almost as tall as Hadley, brought the fug of diesel fuel in with him. Young, with black hair, shaved sides, flat on top, a military cut, a practiced squint. He pointed to Hadley and said, Sit. And Hadley did.

Then he pulled up a chair to the table, sat down himself, elbow up, suspended, fist to his mouth, as if considering a punch, recovering from a punch?

This was stupid, really. All of it. Hadley watched him for another second, then said, Probably a mistake. Right?

For who? You. You have something to say? You'll get your chance. Many in fact.

He was about thirty, pushed in around the nose, like his cheekbones were too small for his face. He looked accustomed to being passed over. Hence the fist.

So, you're in charge?

In charge of you.

He wore a cobbled-together uniform of sorts. Black shirt with buttoned chest pockets, black cotton trousers almost like a carpenter's pants, useful loops and more pockets but no insignia of any kind.

This seems a little improvisational.

Not your high school drama teacher, bud. Bet you wish I was.

Hadley smiled. I need to make a call, he said. Tell my wife and daughter I'll be late.

Go ahead.

Hadley picked up the receiver, still dead. Any court of law, he said, this will go badly for you.

That's funny. But yeah, you should definitely be thinking about a courtroom. Nice and dramatic, right?

5.

Faith might have drawn up a suitable business plan for Jill Marks and if that went well, she'd keep the accounts. That had been the premise of the meeting.

But now Faith couldn't find the next thing to say. Through the new windows, out in the sunny parking lot, Jill Marks's little black coupe looked vulnerable. As if someone must target it for a scratching. Whatever this tremor was, starting in her hands, she usually kept it out of sight, out of her mind. That had always been important. That deferral. But now it was rising in her chest, fluttering. And if she opened her mouth, even for the most perfunctory word she could find, she knew she would say something vile. And she would mean it. But Jill Marks was a silly little girl. Please remember that, Faith told herself. Please. Jill Marks was only a little toy soldier wound up here today by Courtney. Who must be very bored in Upstate New York. That's all. That was all. Same old Courtney Ruddy. Old, old news.

Jill had a smile-and-laugh combo that ruffled across her pretty face like a breeze, then she held it still at the end for a beat. She watched and waited. Smiling.

Faith refolded her legal pad, tried to retract the mechanical pencil, but that didn't work. Moving slowly. Faith's hands were still shaking, and under her arms the dampness felt oily, but Jill Marks kept smiling.

Faith picked up her tote bag and nodded. Now she was formulating a goodbye. It would come to her soon. It would be wise to say something encouraging in her farewell.

But Jill Marks spoke first. She said, Courtney mentioned something about an X factor? When she was setting up the meeting?

Faith waited.

You know, just like at the club? The kids? The ones who can't stay afloat or even breathe right but still get to be in the race. The fragile ones. The X factors. Because everybody gets to be in the race. Isn't that right?

6.

The boom of a plane coming in for a landing, the flight path directly over this room. Everything trembled for a minute, then a blackening shadow rushed over the tarmac. The huge belly of the plane appeared ten feet away before veering up to a sharp left.

Fucking moron.

You're a pilot?

No one lands over here. He's lost.

There was a sustained shuffle outside the door, like the plastic chairs were being quickly rearranged, pushed around. Two voices, then a third, female, which Hadley took for a good sign, irrationally, he thought, and then silence. Ten minutes later, the voices were back and the shuffling. The doorknob jiggled. A rattle of keys and this time the door was opened without force. Mr. Barlow? An airport customer service representative waved at him. A red cap hovered behind her. Mr. Barlow, your wife called to explain our mistake.

She did. Hadley nodded. Good.

That's right, sir. We're terribly sorry.

What the fuck? The man pushed away from the table, raising that wayward fist of his. Get the fuck out of here, he shouted. Both of you. Now.

This way, Mr. Barlow. We'll escort you to your car.

The fuck you will. But the fist dropped and Hadley stood slowly. The woman kept smiling in the door frame. The red cap, a teenager, was smiling, too. Hadley stayed close to the wall until the man stepped aside and hung his head. His chin close to his chest as if in terrible defeat, bested by bland courtesies and a smiling kid. Hadley edged toward the vestibule. He knew from experience how south that feeling could go and how quickly.

Follow me, sir, said the red cap. The door slammed behind them. Just as Hadley passed through the lost luggage, the shouting started—someone else involved now. Then he entered a restricted outdoor area where Boris had the car idling, the briefcase already inside. Hadley fished around for a hundred-dollar bill for the red cap, then dropped down into the back seat of the car. His head sinking into the leather. As if the worst thing had been the insult of a plastic chair. When he took a breath, his lungs fluttered. His trousers felt grimy. He stank of diesel like the angry pilot. The comfort of this seat. This beat-up old car. The cardboard tree dangling from the rearview smelling of fir. He'd told Boris to chuck it a thousand times. But now it smelled like something necessary.

7.

Cece had promised Faith she would be at the house by six. They'd celebrate Faith's birthday after the fact. And since Faith's meeting had ended abruptly and early, there was plenty of time to get ready. How good that Cece was coming down today. What a meeting.

Get a job! That had been her husband Owen's parting shout to her. Get a job. He was weary of her uselessness. And there was no saying back that her use had been incalculable, beyond measure. Endless entertainment for Owen and his brother, Hadley, if nothing else. But there had been a great deal more. Faith knew that. Every day, she thought of Owen. Every day. Something he said or did revving around, digging a groove, before she knew it. Get a job!

But she knew how to peel good advice from a foul delivery. So once Owen was finally settled on his new perch in Hong Kong, she'd gone first to the community college to begin to finish, slowly, at long last, her degree. It took years. But in the end there'd been a lobster dinner to celebrate, Cece eager to begin her own college in the fall, before she, too, left school for an indefinite while. Her mother, Irene, cogent that night, celebratory. Lobsters and very cold white wine. The three of them in a seafood joint on a salt-breezy pier by the ocean. They'd been so happy.

8.

In Owen's stupefying glass box of a living room on Repulse Bay, Hadley spotted the drawing in question on a side table. He might have dropped a drink on top—it was just a scrap of paper—if Owen hadn't glanced up and yelled, Hey, that's the thing! He shuffled over, his hand-embroidered slippers dragging across the stone floor, pulling a frogged silk, black brocade shirt over his belly. Owen tipped the lamp so the bulb shone bright over the tiny sketch.

Hadley didn't know anything about art, but he liked beauty, and there it was.

Owen just wanted him to deliver it, as a love token, to a young trader on the desk at Oppenheimer in New York. It's nothing, said Owen. This is easy.

Hadley, of course, didn't believe him. Eventually, he heard a tall tale about a strapped Moldovan client making partial payment in art. Quite possibly it was a study by Derain. And almost certainly stolen. A smudged and ugly, even bloody, provenance. But in its essence, and this had been Owen's final argument, just a bit of pencil on paper. I could do better. Then do better, Hadley had said.

The small sketch of a woman's breast, the dark dip of an underarm, so, out of the frame the woman's arm was above her head, her body open. Five by seven inches. Owen slipped it into a pink plastic cover, like a kid's last-minute book report. No glassine. No crate.

The problem was the layover. In Paris, Hadley couldn't help himself. He dug the sketch out of his briefcase and brought it to dinner at Chez Rene to show his old friend Anne Wade who knew everything about art. She gasped and said, Under no circumstance was he to take this a step further. He must surrender it immediately. She'd find out how and to whom, so nothing could hurt him, and as soon as she knew, they'd proceed.

I leave the drawing with you, then? said Hadley.

Oh, no.

They kissed each other several times before parting. In the morning, Hadley's head was like an anvil and he was suddenly ready to be home. Awaiting the two o'clock flight at Charles de Gaulle, he had an inkling that to carry the drawing in his briefcase was a mistake. In duty-free he bought a small bright-pink roller bag embossed with the Eiffel Tower in glitter and filled it with souvenir T-shirts and slipped the drawing inside. He wrote "Cecilia" on the ID card and dragged it behind him onto the plane with his duffel wobbling on top. First class was nearly empty, and he slept for most of the Atlantic, but when he woke up, he needed remedies for the terrible head, the aching eyes. The flight attendant was obliging and funny. They arranged to meet for drinks in the city. When they landed, she helped Hadley wrestle the pink thing out of the storage compartment. He looked at it sheepishly and said, Would you mind?

I'm sorry. I really, really can't, she smiled. You know that.

But she pulled the sparkly pink bag right through customs anyway and left it for him by the luggage carousel.

Once they were on the Belt Parkway, Hadley finally asked Boris: Did you get it?

Couldn't touch it.

Was it a tip? Something like that?

Yeah, said Boris. The tip.

And Hadley understood what had happened. Anne Wade at lunch in Paris, telling the important friend, the useful friend, the one who would guide the drawing to safety. She'd talked all about a missing Derain sitting this very minute in a briefcase on Île Saint-Louis. And then she'd picked up her cell phone to tell Hadley the good news. But he was already gone. And Anne Wade could be such a stickler.

Call Belinda or Lindsey. Anyway, she's something at Oppenheimer.

Don't think about it.

No. Hadley looked out and watched the curving swath of the sparkling choppy water, the extravagant sweep, the arc of the Verrazano rising far ahead. Then he closed his eyes, put a hand to his forehead. Owen was a prick. The woman, Belinda, Lindsey, was a toy, nothing. It was the gesture, the extravagance, the danger—for Hadley, that is—that's what puffed him up. It troubled Hadley to know this. After all these years, his brother sometimes seemed like something sticky wedged against his spine. Unseen. Still moving him. So, who called them off? Owen?

No.

So?

It was my mother.

Hadley laughed.

He didn't want to go into the city just yet. Too much nonsense waiting there. While he was in Hong Kong, a newish girlfriend, Petra, had thrown his good pal Lonnie out on the street for no reason. Out of Hadley's place, as if she lived there. And his old girlfriend, now friend, Keko, was threatening violence if he didn't levitate—levitate? he smiled—the German menace out of their life immediately. Their life.

Hadley laughed to think of her. All that lush jealousy. It was something he enjoyed. Maybe even cultivated. Boris looked back at him from the rearview and smiled. Yeah, funny.

The traffic was beginning to choke up. Friday, late afternoon. Everyone eager to leave.

Lonnie would sort himself out, like always. And Petra? Did she deserve the word "menace"? Sometimes she did. He called her Peanut and Pet and then he forgot her name entirely but only when he was very tired.

Let's head down to the shore, said Hadley. The bridge is right there, for godsakes. It's lousy here tonight.

No, no, no, no. Come on! Don't be crazy.

9.

And now that she thought about it, why not? Lobsters. A place on Ocean Avenue sometimes brought them down from Maine on Fridays. She just might get lucky. She'd get a one-pounder for each of them and then a big fat one to make lobster salad to send back to the city with Cece.

What was the very worst thing Jill Marks had said? What had been most insufferable? She wished she could call Owen right now and say, Oh, you wouldn't believe! And the thread that stayed alive would tighten and knot to hear him. Hear him dismiss her slipping, wading into the thick dark past. Then he'd rush right off the line. Busy. He wrote to her but not often. She'd received a postcard around her birthday. Fifty-nine this year. How did she already know he'd forget sixty?

But the image was a woman, a redhead, by Derain. Something rare and gorgeous was all the card said, but of course she knew his handwriting. Once her mother had asked her—but this was during the last, batty phase—she'd asked: How was Owen in bed? Faith had guffawed, then said to her own surprise: Not great. Well, you always had Hadley for all that, said Irene. Not a bit! said Faith. Not once. Are you crazy? But Irene was not crazy.

Every once in a great while, Hadley still showed up in some rattrap of a town car, a thug of a driver at the wheel. Last time she'd felt him coming, almost a premonition. She was in the yard, thinning the cosmos seedlings she'd planted around a downed tree. A bit of fluttery pink to mask a raw stump. She looked up and saw the hideous car, this time a hornet-green color, and she walked right up to the end of the drive and stood, straddle legged, with a spade tight in one fist.

Hadley nodded at her from the back seat, one bump up of his famous chin, exactly the same. He had the decency, she thought later, not to smile. The car continued down the road. And that was that. That would always be that. What was insufferable? All of it.

But when Cece was a baby, when the summer was high and hot, the ocean was in the air all the time, like something to touch, Faith lay out naked in the yard on the grass, with the baby on her belly in the dead of night and watched the stars. Neither could sleep. Cece gurgled and sputtered, and Faith patted her tiny back, her rump. Faith's belly still as squishy as a jellyfish and Cece paddled and swam. The two of them on the warm grass under the stars. The screen door creaked opened—she thought it was Owen—but it was Hadley who lay down beside her and put his mouth to her cheek just to taste her, just the once, and then he rested there beside them. Every once in while he hummed.

HOW THE POETS
LEARNED TO LOVE HER

I n the middle was the horror of her sister's death. Her younger sister had been a thoughtful woman. Kind to their mother. Or was it a stepmother? But when she was alive a secret disappointment because she hadn't amounted to much. It was embarrassing. Though once someone crosses the threshold of forty—and here there'd come a shrug—and the poets, who thought this "older" sister interesting, bracing, refreshing, and so young, shrugged, too, and smiled. What did they know about forty. They were facing bigger thresholds, unimaginable.

This bracing, refreshing sister, married now to their oldest friend, was good at provisions. That's what her husband said, *procurement*. The old poet called her Madame, which was sly and sexy. But he confided to the other poets, when she was out in the kitchen, whipping things up, that she wasn't interested in sex. Not like he was. Not at all.

But she told them when her younger sister's marriage of only a single year fell apart, to a woman brought home only *after* the wedding—so, there were many surprises—the mother or was it a stepmother had made it very clear what she thought of this jowly person with the greenish hair. No need to speak. No discussion. After that single visit home, the new spouse, Priscilla, wept all the way back to Memphis.

A few weeks later, the younger sister returned alone to the house where they'd grown up in Long Branch on Honeysuckle Lane. The stepmother—it *was* a stepmother, a *Ruth* no less— still lived there, her home décor practice conducted in the paneled den where the girls had once watched westerns on the television, lolling on the sofa, on the floor. With snacks. The younger sister was that spoiled, that loved as a child. Maybe even a bit more than the older one. The stepmother, who now closed the louvered doors for her clients, had loved the younger one best, they felt sure. Though the surprise spouse—weeping Priscilla, the old poet dubbed her—had other ideas.

The note she left for the stepmother was passed around and amended, edited, lengthened by the poets. What the original note said was: *Please drink your coffee on the back porch this morning.* It was written with a rollerball on a white-lined index card—a combination she liked to use for her work, when she was working. She enjoyed the crisp clarity. The no nonsense. She'd been, lately, a saleswoman of office furniture. It was pressured competitive work, and later the poets would hear from the older sister, a hotbed of drug abuse. Almost an occupational hazard.

Please drink your coffee on the back porch this morning. So much consideration. The stepmother's routine—the index card writer had imagined—would only be disrupted for the one day. From the back porch, which overlooked a fenced back garden and was hemmed by cyprus and hemlock and holly— evergreens dense, overgrown—she was to see nothing but her own backyard. And the sound of the emergency teams, if they were lazy and slow at their work, would be muffled, too. The coffeepot was on a timer. The card writer imagined—the poets were of one mind on this—that her remains would be scooped up and transported far from Honeysuckle Lane long before the coffee began its first noisy percolation. The younger sister's plan—and the older sister was angry, so angry that for a while her dinners declined—was to lie down on the roadbed in the dark and let a car, or cars, ride over her, as if no one would notice! The streetlights were inadequate to that kind of blackness. Her body would be just another slender line laid down.

*　*　*

The older sister believed she'd begun shooting drugs the year before the end. This was the central problem, she said. The impetus. Priscilla's doing. Priscilla wasn't invited to the funeral. The old poet reported the details of this tiny terrible private occasion to his friends: The stepmother's chignon fell crooked over the black collar of her dress. Pins falling. His eyes widened, and the poets smiled at him, tracing his thought. The curve of that falling hair.

There'd been no argument from the priest in Long Branch, at Star of the Sea, about consecrated ground. The sister was buried next to her sainted father. The stepmother made sure of that. But fairly soon after the burial, the old poet's young wife began distributing her valuables among the friends for safekeeping.

Why? they asked.

And she looked at them with tearful eyes, and they were struck dumb.

The poets were struck, that is, not the wives and partners, the long sufferers as they called themselves in friendly solidarity. The poets saw a change in her, something more likable than her beef cuts and right wineglasses. Yes, she'd changed. And the poets didn't mention this to her husband—the old poet, their dear old friend—because they knew how that would go. And they didn't discuss it with the long sufferers

either. The ones who had the day jobs and the health insur-
ance. Or with each other, really, for a while. But each poet
had his own private experience of receiving a well-wrapped
package on a late afternoon. A wintry sunset already purpling
the sky. The spruce a sharp and bitter blue. She wore a per-
fume for these errands. They all laughed when this fact was
disclosed later. She smelled like pine soap and a bit of good
fucking all at once. It was heady and subliminal until they
talked about it. And it made this passing of the brown wrapped
package—her jewels? her documents?—more exciting, and
it inclined them to secrecy. But the tears and the look in her
sad eyes that she counted on them—men who by everything
they held dear were sworn unreliable—this is what made
them loyal. Very loyal.

Later they tried to piece it together. A time line. Maybe it really
did begin that late winter just after the poor sister's death, the
February with the doorstep packages and the purple light. The
sad brimming eyes and the smell of nice fucking under the
bushes beside a newly paved road. Maybe that was when their
petted, prosaic, and occasionally still bloodred bedmates first
became expendable. But not all of them at first. The divide
was drawn quietly, neatly. They just didn't see it.

The following year their old friend, the oldest poet, had a spring-
time death and that was right and sweet. The wives, partners,

children, friends, fellow poets and artists, they loved him now for his excessive ways. The trysts, the serial negligence, the torqueing devotion to his children, followed always by a sharp rebalancing dose of vicious madness. Yes, they all loved him, because the trysts were long ago. And nowadays would be nothing. Nothing! The negligence, swept up and patched by all the many refractive newer days. The children long grown interesting and durable in adulthood. They only saw his beauty now: his roar was beautiful, his crying unanswerable need something deep and pure. No longer destroying or perverted or blind. They loved him, they surrounded his wide white bed, they surrendered their hearts as they always had to the greatness of his endeavors. This endeavor. All along.

His young widow took a different view. Now the divesting was sweeping, immediate, and large. No more furtive packages in twilight. One of the wives, already questionable, said the body was barely cool before the holy bed was wrapped in decontaminating plastic and standing on end, leaning against the garage doors, out in the drive. A new fresh bed delivered by nightfall. The poets didn't believe this slander, though the phrase "new bed" bounced by very briefly and was jotted down by one or two to be considered later.

Their beloved old poet gone from this world, and there was his sad widow, head bowed on the threshold, lifting an arm to point, briefly, over there. Then dropping it again, stuffing both hands in the front pocket of her black hoodie. She was so young, the poets said to one another. It was what they could most read in the gesture. What they could each easily, easily imagine. Of course she needs a new bed.

One of the wives, a long sufferer, a loudmouth, said, I'll tell you what I see. Here's what I think the gesture says: She'd like to take that sweeping, pointing arm and brush it over that entire house, all of it, and make it her very own. Now. Out with the books, the posters, the tributes, the prizes, the letters, for godsakes, the letters. She needs to erase and burn the hard drives. She needs a bonfire—at least—for the videos. A bonfire, a dumpster, a rat-infested garbage heap. A river of shit.

The poets stared. This particular wife had always been reactive.

She needs to burn the fucking place down. Get a court order. A bulldozer. She needs a plane to fly overhead and douse the place with a fungicide. And when she's done—when the place is burned and dug up to the foundations and deloused and disinfected, when it's no longer a superfund of his depravity—maybe then, she'll have another holiday party. Or give you her secret packages. But don't hold your breath. See what I mean?

*   *   *

They did not. Would not. This loudmouth wife was being unkind.

But like a line or a track was being laid carefully, invisibly, beneath them, the poets—who had long loved the partners, the wives, their earth-stomping dayworkers as much as they loved their own lusty heads in the stars—the poets gradually lost purchase there. They lost the thread. They were pulled in a different direction now.

All the poets and certainly the young widow ignored the outburst from the loudmouth. But years later, when the poets tried to remember, when they were willing to discuss it, they had to acknowledge, just provisionally—because hadn't she always been trouble?—this particular wife was the first to go. She had to go.

But why? Well. They didn't know.

Was it the first Christmas Eve? No, the second. The young widow was expected momentarily. They'd made the place cozy and gentle. Soothing. The poets had each, privately, made a luminaria to light her way along the dark path through the spruce trees. And there they all were, the paper lanterns popping up out of the snow. They'd written a verse or two. Also privately. Secreted in a special pocket. Right at the tips of their wondering fingers. But as the dinner cooled and the fire banked, the luminaria sputtered and the spruce went black, the loudmouth wife stood behind them on the back doorstep where they stood together, waiting, and she said, All of you, inside now. She's not coming.

Not so, said the poets.

Look, she's not. Why would she?

They frowned.

Listen. She took advantage of her husband's fame. She used his connections, including you. She flaunted his good name, while whispering about the more repulsive aspects of his character. She hoarded his money and kept it from his children. She changed the will. She changed the deed. She changed the name on the final manuscript. She altered the driveway, the front walk, the front door. She took over his office and made it her own. She went to an artist colony because suddenly she's the writer and took up his board seat, too. Now she's an expert on artists and writers. Why would she need to come here?

That loudmouth! She was awful!

* * *

Just a game, sweetheart, and she's good at it. It was the last of her observations.

Very unkind.

Maybe three or four years after the old poet died, the remaining poets received a group email from Italy. The young widow was staying on at the American Academy in Rome. She'd been granted an extension, her work deemed too valuable to let slip away. Her extension was in fact indefinite. She'd been offered the same suite of rooms as B— And here she demurred. I'm not worthy.

She's really not! the loudmouth might have said, but she wasn't on the thread. No one knew where *she* was these days. Some of the other long sufferers were gone, too, by now. Discarded. Some were only disaffected.

The poets had all written letters of support and they were gratified to hear the young widow was doing so well, but she did have one tiny request, since she couldn't possibly leave Rome now: the stepmother.

*   *   *

And maybe this is where the story begins. If the younger sister was the terrible middle, and the old poet, seen at long last through the eyes of love, was the end, then this, the poets began to believe—and it frightened them in its starkness—might be the start.

Who picked her stepmother up at the train station? They all did.

A huddle of poets, braced against the whipping wind off the icy river, sheltered only by each other's warmth. The train crept in to a stop. They already felt the escaped curl on the collar. The sexy wisp. As if the old poet had bequeathed them something delicious. Alive. Breathing.

So they were facing the wrong direction looking up when a single rider disembarked. The stooped woman dragged her roller case right by them. A catch in one wheel, a shriek and a yank. It was too heavy a bag and if the poets thought to help, as they might ordinarily, at the moment they had a higher calling.

They waited. One poet turned just in time to glimpse the elevator doors closing on the woman in the red knit cap, blowing her nose on a shred of tissue. He looked back up at the stilled train. Waiting. Something was wrong. The idling engine hissed to silence. The reek of creosote filled the air. Inside a crackled announcement. The poets strained forward to hear.

The train, they heard, was disabled. But everyone should keep their seats. No one was to move. Strange instructions, the poets all thought. But then uniformed police were sweeping over the platform, prying open every door, entering every car by force. And now the poets themselves were pressed for identification.

What for? Wait. What's wrong?

They were herded as one up the stairs and shoved right out of the station. The doors cordoned off behind them. They could scarcely make sense of the horror they felt rising, and more than one poet felt on the verge of tears, real tears. What could they do? What was happening? But they'd already seen the very worst in their imaginations. Many times. They knew. They knew.

Looking for me? The old woman in the red knit cap, tapping her nose with the tissue shred, sat quite straight now on the stone wall near the paved empty car lot, her heavy bag tipped sideways. Wheels entirely broken. Crushed. Bent. Not going one more turn. Above them the sky went black and starless. Below the train was still. Looking for me? she said again. And they were. And they understood then that they were. That much, so far, seemed obvious.

CALIFORNIA

O ona wasn't budging. Her father leaned down for a private conference away from the clutch of mothers on the playground. Oona Claire? he said in a serious whisper.

She turned her head away and growled but quietly.

Arthur stood up, stretched his long arms. The school would close its gates soon, and all the mothers were putting away the fruit leather and the juice boxes. Afterschool play was done for the day, but Oona's love, William, still hadn't emerged from the building.

He's in trouble, said Oona.

What kind of trouble? said Arthur, sitting back down on the railroad tie bench, waving to the successfully departing parents. His wave said, my life is impossible, and the other parents gave polite smiles. He asked too much was the unstated consensus.

William hates his cubby, said Oona.

Okay?

He *really* likes music.

This was a threadbare topic. Oona was good on the rhythm triangle, better than Oona T. She could bang hard enough to get the *brrring*. Loud!

Arthur dropped his head between his hands. Then his phone vibrated against his heart. He dug it out to scan. Angie the babysitter was canceling for tonight because of her boyfriend's cold. Fuck me, he said, then looked around. But the place was deserted except for Oona, who was guarding the path between the door and the gate.

Come on, beast. Ice cream. Then you put on a dress and we'll head over to Nathan's book party.

Nathan wrote a book?

Nathan wrote a novel. You know that, Oona. Come on, tushy in the stroller.

Not *this* minute, said Oona. A new phrase she was testing. She ambled closer to the school door, letting herself be catchable. A straight run would be an outrage. This way she was still clear of an argument. Cece the play therapist had talked to Oona about defiance and where it led. Lately she and her father were on a better footing, and Cece said Oona's good attitude was the spark. Cece had big lips with points she liked to color pink.

There he is! Oona jumped up and down, shouting her father over.

But Arthur was busy typing a plea to Angie the babysitter to rescue him just once more and he would make it worth her while. Bargaining. Begging. He shook the phone as if he could speed up her response. Oona held herself in a shivering hug.

Oona? Over here. Now.

William's nanny backed out the double doors, angling the stroller so as not to bang his feet. His boots were tied together and flung over the nanny's shoulder infantry style. He wore red-striped socks and a green eye patch over his left eye. William had been born with a rare ptosis in one eye. His other eye, his mother, Rachel, assured the school, was perfect, in fact superior to most eyes, and her resistance to any kind of special ed track for William was titanic. One afternoon, Arthur had watched Rachel wrestle the head teacher, Miss Sarah, to near tears and felt a familiar jab at the base of his spine. Just where he preferred to ignore it. Shit, he'd said to no one as Rachel made her way swiftly, triumphantly— William stumbling behind her—to the town car at the curb. No black SUV for Rachel. The man opening the door wore a cap. When Arthur reported all this to his friend Nathan, there was no need to explain the impact of the scene. Rachel was a movie star.

Now William's nanny watched the way out like she was navigating hostile terrain. Oh, Oona, she said. Not today.

And Oona wanted to know: Why?

This William, said the nanny. He is in the mood to be home in his room thinking over what he said to Miss Sarah just now. Isn't that right, William?

William knocked his head back against the stroller, then yawned.

Are you tired, William? asked Oona. Bad dreams?

William looked at Oona and smiled a sleepy tenderness.

221

All right, lovebirds, said the nanny. Good day, Oona.

She wheeled William out of the little playground, while Oona tapped her toes—one, two—then did as graceful a leap as her small pink parka would allow. She was a dancer, just like her mother.

Tomorrow if William is still in a bad mood? I'll give him some crayons, Oona said, letting her father strap her into the stroller now. The stroller was a big concession lately brokered by Cece the play therapist. Oona at four could easily outwalk her father. But as long as William used one, Oona wanted one, too. And Cece said maybe the security of the stroller wasn't a bad idea while the mother was still away from the home.

Try away from the planet, said Arthur and got a recalibrating smile in return.

Immediately, Oona confirmed that her mother was in California, which *was* still on the planet, right?

Her father said, that's right. He was sorry. He'd made a mistake. And the next time Cece offered suggestions: regular mealtimes for Oona, a vegetable or two, scheduled weekly communication with the mother, he just nodded. Open. Learning.

Right now he was learning patience. Plugging then replugging the inscrutable straps into the right sockets on the stroller. His phone vibrated again. He stood up and pressed it to his ear, making the shush sign to Oona.

Jesus, Angie, you're my savior. No, that's perfect. I'll give you the address and you can pick her up there and then get her some dinner. I'll be home early. You'll only miss a sneeze or two. No, no, no, I'm grateful! You're a rock star.

* * *

This very week at play therapy, Cece had said that sometimes dreams are like stories and Oona could color her dreams with crayons to read them. So Oona drew a gray squirrel with a pink strawberry hat and said, That's Mommy coming home.

Cece said, Very nice. *Very* nice. Then she asked about the coiled-looking brown cloud at the top. Now, where's that sunshine hiding?

A question Oona loved because William's nanny often said something very similar. Where was her sunshine boy hiding? Where was the lovely sunshine boy she knew? When Oona reported all this to her father—the squirrel, the coil, the excellent sunshine question—he shook his head but kept his mouth shut. They were both trying hard, he finally said. You and me, Oona, giving it the old elbow grease.

And Oona loved this, too, because elbow grease was how her father got through law school, that and the galvanizing foreboding that her mother would be the expensive kind of love.

At first, when Oona's mother had gone to Arizona for just a smidgen of rehabilitation, her father had stayed nearby in a rip-off hotel and tried very hard to help. Then he needed to come home to Oona and to his job. The minute he left, Oona's spacy aunt Sally, her mother's older sister, flapped in to assess the situation. She'd found a better, reputable, really medical, really spiritual place in California. So she packed up Oona's mother and flew her to San Francisco and moved her—just for the moment—into the two-bedroom pool house in Russian Hill. Near family, close to home.

What about this fucking family? This fucking home? Arthur had said, or something along those lines, questions he would ask again and again. Then he caught the next red-eye.

If anything, she seemed more gone than ever and that made her tender with him, that and the wide dark-purple sky and the sparkling pool. For one night they nestled in a bed that smelled like fresh bamboo and excellent weed and he whispered into her sleeping ear: Come back.

But the next Monday morning back in New York her sister, Sally, called him at work to say the visit hadn't helped. The doctors felt the relationship needed to cool down a tad.

The doctors said "tad"?

Then some medical student was cued to join the call for a consultation. The upshot? No more visits. For the time being. And the family would now foot the bills. Going forward, Sally said. As if that settled everything.

At the time, Arthur told his friend Nathan that rehab is rehab. Either she cleans up or she doesn't. The Napa Valley didn't have any special edge. Really she could be doing this in Queens. And that could be the possible next step. After California knocked itself out.

Outpatient, inpatient. Eventually the pool house became awkward, so an old friend offered a guest cottage in their vineyard. Outpatient, inpatient. Then a cousin had a carriage house he didn't need for the moment. Inpatient, outpatient, inpatient. Three months, six months, nine months, a year, and so far, Arthur was right about California.

But at Cece's suggestion, on Sunday evenings, if her father was home and her mother felt up to it and Oona was quick in her bath, the plan was to Skype her mother. This happened once. Mommy, Daddy pointed out, could be hard to track down.

But on this special night her mother's face filled up her father's computer screen and Oona's face was in a tiny stamp in the corner.

Mama? Oona said to the screen.

Yes, baby? said her mother.

Do you remember how to get here? Oona knew this had been a problem in the past.

I always know where you are, kitty cat, said her mother. Then she made a movement outside the screen. Someone in a dim corner in California needed her mother to go rest now. Then the screen blooped dark.

Is Mommy in trouble?

Arthur began tapping through Netflix for a treat. Why, sweetheart?

Going to bed early?

Mommy's a little bit sick, remember? He tapped his forehead. It's in Mommy's mind. And being with Aunt Sally is like being captured by a poisonous gelatinous space alien.

Oona's eyes went wide.

I'm joking! Joking. Anyway, it makes her very tired, Oona.

Are you tired, Daddy?

Oh, just every single minute of every single day.

And then the room went still. He slid a glance at her.

Right away, no warning, Oona opened her mouth wide and began to howl. She shrieked.

Hey! Arthur said. What the hell?

Oona yelled louder, a weird warbling keen that stung his ears. Stop it! Oona! Cut it out.

But she couldn't stop. The more she yelled, the more it was impossible to cut it out.

Oh my god. Shut up! he said, but she kept going. Louder and louder.

Even when his hand flew right up in front of her face—so fast, too fast for both of them—even then she couldn't stop. But he'd caught his hand just in time, and he stayed that way holding his right hand with his left, frozen, until he started to cry, too.

There was luck in this. And for a half second in some barely known way he understood he hadn't always been so lucky. He said, Please, please, stop. But he was whispering now, not making any attempt to quiet her. Soon the neighbors would be knocking on the door. The walls were practically rice paper. Who the fuck cared? Really. Who the fuck cared? Shriek away, Oona. Shriek away.

At last a pause.

He peeked to see her hand splayed and round on her red wet cheek, patting, patting, patting. Her triangle rhythm, the one William liked best. One, two, three. And.

Oh, Oona. Oona.

He kissed the top of her head. Then he stood up to get some water from the kitchen. His in the Mets plastic beer tumbler, hers in the preferred plain green shot glass. He sat back down on the sofa beside her and looked through the computer. His T-shirt smelled filthy even to him. Then he perked up and said, Holy cow!

When she didn't respond, he said, Wow. This is fantastic.

What? Oona finally said. What is, Daddy?

Only our favorite, he said. Starting this minute! Thus surrendering once again to the magical power of *The Searchers*.

Oona didn't really care for *The Searchers*. But her father settled his laptop on her mother's old embroidered meditation cushion. He only liked certain parts of the movie. The things really worth watching. Encore? he'd say after an especially mighty scene.

At bedtime, as usual, they counted the dopey flat green sheep on her duvet cover. Good, she said. Just like her mother, Oona was quick to forgive.

And Arthur was trying his best, too. He answered the ritual questions about California and her mother's imminent return. He put on a friendly face and that's all that was needed. Goodnight. But they both knew that for him the upset would need to harden in some way then find a release in verbal darts to come. Comments aimed to solidify and eject the misery he now felt only at the base of his throat. Even with the pink T. rex night-light aglow and grape-scented bath soap in the air. Oona's lips pursed like a cartoon angel in presleep. Goodnight. And still he couldn't stop the lash of anger but only at his throat, and that was a big improvement.

Cece the play therapist was all about Oona, but she liked to give Arthur pointers when she felt she could safely lob one in. Stuff about breathing and feeling his body. Her latest? Anger like his didn't just pack up and go away. Pack up? Anyway, who said he was angry?

Well. Miss Sarah, the preschool head teacher, for one. Her classroom assistant, Miss Peg. It was the unanimous unspoken consensus of the parents on the playground. His old friend Nathan, occasionally, but like the waiting mothers at dismissal, it didn't really bother him much. For them it was more a noticeable quality—the whole quivering high-frequency affect—than a problem.

For Oona's mother, it had been a problem. One she solved with white wine and Klonopin in the early days. Later, after the baby was born—a tough delivery, an arduous recovery—a new world of opportunity opened up. And with her opportunity came opposition in Arthur. And this opposition, eventually, brought the neighbors knocking, sometimes calling through the door, and when that didn't work, they went down to the lobby and started buzzing. Once they called the police. It was an unfair fight. Oona's mother could fade away to black at will. And then Arthur was left alone with all that terrible, terrible fury.

Coursing through the blood, said Cece, as if all fury were identical and biological. She made her hands move like two fish swimming in unison. Feisty fish who may feel good and exciting but created misery and discord wherever they swam in Arthur's system. His pounding heart? His migraine headaches? His teeth. Naturally, from that moment on, Arthur had his ears open—where the fish were especially seductive—for a new play therapist.

Early in the new year, it came to light that Oona didn't like to answer questions in preschool. When Arthur asked her why not, she said it was because she didn't know the answers. He said she only needed to think a little and the answer would pop into her mind, right behind her eyes.

Just like in Mommy's mind?

Well, everyone has their own kind of mind, sort of. You know that, he said. Let's practice. What's your name?

Oona!

What's my name?

Arthur!

What's our best bud's name?

Nathan!

And your play therapist?

Oona waited. Oona waited a little more, and her father nodded. Oona looked into her mind. Mommy loves me in her heart?

That's right, he said. Totally right.

And they didn't practice anymore after that.

* * *

In moments of sorrow, weariness, elation, loneliness, and everyday frustration Arthur sometimes still believed that Oona's mother also loved him in her heart. Late in the night his phone would vibrate and he'd bring it deep under the covers, old covers, same covers, for long talks drenched in impossibility. Sometimes she was the impossible one. But not always, he knew that. He loved, most of all, to hear the first rasp of irritation rise close inside his ear. Her first cracked note. That, then the cool switchback. The barb, the bite, the swift crazy sock of joy. Then it was a race to who could hang up first. Then all the black hours to follow. Pointless, tuneless, exhausted walks to school, to the office. Then one day, she was back in her sister Sally's pool house, and the calls stopped for good. The account disconnected.

When Arthur dialed the big house in daylight, Sally didn't know what he was talking about.

Of course she hadn't taken away the phone! Anyway, she was just about to touch base with Arthur to arrange for a visit from Oona. She was getting her ducks in a row. Then she'd FedEx Oona's plane ticket. Okay?

You fucking space odyssey. Oona's not flying to California on her own. She's four. Okay? You and your bullshit chitchat, Arthur said, or something along those lines. Then he slammed the phone on his desk.

Surprisingly, Sally phoned Arthur back. She needed him to hear this directly from her. Going forward, all communications would be between the lawyers. Got it? Maybe the kind of chitchat Arthur could understand. At least the only kind he'd ever get from this family again. Then she made an obscene little buzz deep in her throat. And Arthur felt his own throat dissolve in something deeper than anger or disgust, something obliterating, something maybe permanent.

Long, long ago, just like Oona's, William's parents had been married, too. But only briefly. During the first of William's many operations, his father had failed to show up at the pediatric surgical wing in a timely way. When he did swing by for a visit he found Rachel's lawyer in the waiting room with the documents. Everyone on the playground knew this story. Now William lived with his mother on West Tenth Street and on alternate Tuesdays he and his nanny were delivered in the town car for an overnight at his father's.

All her life Oona had lived in only one place, on East Eighteenth Street, now with just Arthur. This had been true since last spring, and now it was nearly spring again. Over and over, Oona suggested to her father, to Nathan, to Cece, and even to Angie the babysitter that they should all just go live in California instead. But no one thought this was a good idea. Mommy needed rest, they all said. Then one day, early in March, Nathan brought over a special Chinese dinner. After the first bite, her father had news, and the news was divorce. Just like William's parents!

Oona closed her eyes.

But wait. That meant she could see Mommy now, right? Just like William did?

Of course, said Nathan.

Eventually, said her father. He waved around, indicating a mountain of stuff that would need collecting.

Oona followed the motion of his hand. Mommy's coming? Here? Now?

Sweetheart, what does eventually mean?

Oona, love bug, your mother is *wonderful*, said Nathan, nodding hard.

Just like Nathan, Oona's mother had been a fiction writer, but only momentarily. She'd signed up for Nathan's workshop at the Ninety-Second Street Y: Put Your Body into Words. All her life, she'd been a dancer. Now she just might find her way to something new. Immediately, Nathan told Arthur she was the most gifted student in the class, which was code for the most beautiful.

Listen up, said Nathan. Your mother has a rare, deeply intuitive way of knowing.

And that's really what we're talking about here, said Arthur into his Mets cup.

Exquisite mind, said Nathan. He banged the ketchup bottle bottom hard over his noodles. And Oona started to shiver, always a prelude to disaster.

Oh! Mommy's a seeker, all right, said her father, shaking a splattering brown chicken hunk on his chopsticks close up to his eyes, as if something horrible and death dealing was attacking his face. Then he let it attack Oona for a moment before putting it down and pulling her in close. Come on, knucklehead. You'll see Mommy sooner than you know.

Oona leaned against her father's chest but stiffly.

Come on. Where's my ferocious beast? Huh? He shook her softly until finally, obligingly, in semibeast mode, Oona clawed the sweet orangey glob on his T-shirt. There she is. There's my worst nightmare.

Then Nathan scavenged in the kitchen for other condiments. There was loose talk about strawberry cupcakes hiding in a bag and maybe even a select viewing of *The Searchers*.

And what did the play therapist Cece recommend when she heard the news? A date.

I'm sorry. What? said Arthur.

She threw up her hands as if to say: What, a date would kill you? I think you'll find a lot has evolved in the last year. Am I out of line?

Of course you're out of line. Arthur shook his head in wonder. He looked to Oona, who wasn't listening.

Wait a minute, he said. Wait. Are you saying there's a reward?

A reward? No, Arthur. Don't be ridiculous, Cece laughed.

But now Arthur was the one not listening.

Earliest spring and it was completely obvious what a reward, an upgrade might look like. On the nanny's next day off, Arthur struck up a conversation with William's mother, Rachel, on the playground.

Right away Oona could see that Rachel didn't know the answer to her father's question. Rachel frowned and turned away and watched the sidewalk until her driver pulled up with the town car, then she placed delicate blue-gloved hands around her pale pink mouth and called out to William in her celebrated voice: Come on, Silly-Billy. Andiamo.

That was the first time. Two weeks later, when Arthur spoke to Rachel, he began by talking very fast, as if her ears were already closing. She kept a stern, frozen face behind her immense sunglasses—one of her very best expressions. So Arthur hunched over his knees, hands clasped between his shins and whispered to Rachel in tortured, halting phrases, the haiku version of Oona's mother's desertion.

(I didn't actually use that word, of course, he told Nathan later.)

Then he mentioned *The Searchers*, just to open up a little common ground, and Rachel laughed. One loud, help-less bark. She called out to William in a completely different voice, Billy Boy? Angel love. Time's up.

Angel love? The magnolia trees with their squirrel-fur buds still clung to the building for warmth. But if nothing else was willing to bloom, a fresh intelligence began to emerge on the playground: Arthur showed up. Anger issues? Sure. Needy? Without question. But there he was, day after day, and everyone began to acknowledge that. And he felt it. He believed his shift in status had seeped all the way out to the town car. That's what Rachel's new voice said to him. Angel.

Love. Loud and clear, Arthur reported to Nathan. Recognition. Respect. Definitely respect.

Maybe you need a new venue? said Nathan.

What's a venue? said Oona.

The first week of April, when William visited his father, his nanny, as always, slept in the cubby-like room off the kitchen. And William, as always, crept out of his own bed, put on his boots, and crawled under the nanny's foldaway cot and slept there instead.

The next afternoon, wintry cold, Oona huddled next to William's nanny on the railroad tie bench and ate mango slices. William dozed in the stroller.

Little boy up half the night, no wonder he sleep in school, said the nanny. She shook her head, her thick big turban. Oona put out a hand to touch it. Not with those sticky mitts, said the nanny and found a wipe in William's backpack. It was getting close to five and most of the mothers were preparing to go home. But Arthur hadn't arrived yet.

Your daddy probably has a business problem, said the nanny. We'll give him a little longer, then ask Miss Sarah for advice. The nanny laughed at this and woke William. Right away William started to cry.

Our William is hungry, said the nanny, and she pulled a smile shape of mango out of the plastic bag. No need for tears.

But William only pushed the mango away and cried harder. Oona covered her face the way her father sometimes did. In this disguise she bent down and kissed William's hand. Seriously, thoughtfully.

There you are, Oona, kissing away the little cloud to make my sunshine appear.

William ignored this but stopped crying. He breathed rapidly, watching Oona with his sad uncovered eye.

You're a good girl, Oona. I'll say that. Now, where's your daddy got to today. He's usually right on time.

Miss Sarah came out and began to lock the school door behind her. Miss Sarah had a long gray braid as thick as a horse's tail. To match her face, Daddy said and then made Oona promise to never repeat that. Miss Sarah wrapped her horsey face tight in a thin red scarf and walked straight over to the nanny.

Arthur just called to say he's been held up at the office. And I have a dentist appointment, said Miss Sarah. He wondered, and I wonder— Could you possibly?

I understand, Miss Sarah, said the nanny as if she were talking to William. I understand. She nodded her head up and down to coax Miss Sarah into the right answer. She knew it, if she'd just think a little.

Miss Sarah finally said, Okay. I'll try to reach Miss Peg.

Thank you, said the nanny. Just for today, William, let's wear these pretty boots home.

Straight to voice mail, said Miss Sarah, sighing. And I really can't stay. She put her hand around her jaw.

Oona, come home! said William. And when his nanny frowned, he added: Please!

Shall I call Rachel for permission?

The nanny shook her head but said, Yes, Miss Sarah, please do that. And then she patted Oona's hand so she wouldn't get the wrong idea. Wouldn't think she wasn't welcome. Where are your gloves, Oona? I know your daddy didn't send you to school with no gloves.

It was nearly dark by the time they reached West Tenth Street, and William and Oona were very tired, but they didn't cry. When they climbed up the stoop to the front door, the nanny used her key to get inside. The house was dim, and there was a note from the housekeeper on the front hall table. The nanny's forehead wrinkled when she read it, then she said, Coats! Let's march! And Oona and William were soldiers all the way to the closet. Oona's parka got a special wooden hanger rounded on both ends. To the mess hall, said the nanny. March!

William led the way down to the kitchen, where Oona and William sat together on the banquette while the nanny heated the soup and buttered the crackers. Oona's legs pointed straight out on the polka-dot cushion, but William sat on the very edge and teetered.

I've never seen such sleepy soldiers, said the nanny, and she put the warm soup in blue-and-white bowls on the table. She gave them each a Chinese spoon, which was bigger than Oona's mouth. Pretend it's a cup, William said. The crackers were crumbly. The soup was milky. The dark kitchen had a smell like dry cleaning, sour and small. No wonder William slept so much. He was dozing off again now and the nanny was busy grinding spices with a rock and Oona was a little bit sad. So she told the nanny the soup was good. I like it! But the spoon was too strange for her, so she picked up the bowl, which was slippery.

Rachel entered the front door on West Tenth Street peacefully. A white noise machine she'd had fitted into the wall of the foyer like a minispeaker said Wave, said Sand, but not like in New Jersey or god forbid California, more Bali on the unspoiled side of the island. Slim, slow-moving transparent waves, sand-tickling waves. It was a lovely feeling and the sound brought the blue and green colors of the foyer into order. Rachel took a deep breath and smelled the awful chicken soup coming up from the lower level. The architects had tried and tried, but there was no masking the traveling scents in an old house, so she'd fired them.

Moving to the closet, she saw a small pink ratty down jacket. Strange. Then she remembered the message relayed from Miss Sarah and right on schedule pain split her head, pulsing like a heartbeat: pain, pain, pain. As if at the end of a stupendously stupid day she could possibly be okay. As if she could spend precious hours of her life taped into a fur bikini (yes, she got the reference) teaching her mortal enemies yoga and then chopping off their heads once they were relaxed.

The story made no sense. This little pulsing fragment of her brain was all she had left, and it was crying uncle.

She made her way down the back stair toward the chicken soup smell—the cloves, the coriander, the cinnamon—for yet another word with the nanny. William couldn't sleep as it was. The spices, come on. She was figuring out how to phrase this tactfully when she caught sight of the messy little girl from school.

And then—so quickly!—Rachel was on the floor. Ow, she said.

Missus Rachel, said the nanny. Are you all right?

She had that implacable expression that Rachel loathed on anyone really but especially in her own home.

It's all fine, now, said the nanny, nodding. Isn't that so.

And Rachel didn't know what she was talking about. She was sitting in soup. The floor, the cushions, William. The soup was everywhere. And the stink! She'd never get it out. What was fine?

She took a brief eyes-only glance around, as she did when a film set had gone berserk. It seemed like someone had half thrown her there. This happened on set, too. Improvisations, followed by lawsuits. She used the table—slimy—as a ballet barre and did a deep plié off the floor, moving as if she still wore the fur bikini and none of the tape to preserve her privacy could be relied on. She was standing, good. She began to speak, but then, no. Oh, no. That would happen later. Instead, she was nodding. And she was exiting.

Rachel made it all the way up into the master suite and stripped right down to the skin. She had itchy gray tape gum on her inner thighs. Her shins were oily orange with soup spice. Obviously, the nanny had to go. First thing tomorrow. Right now, these foul sopping stinking clothes could be kicked straight out the bedroom door—there. Done. Finito.

Downstairs, the doorbell jangled just like the notes of Oona's brass triangle. The nanny stepped carefully around the spilled soup and went to the kitchen door. She unlocked the gate and called up to the sidewalk: Hello? May I help you? She strained to see who was standing above on the stoop.

Hey! It's me! Looking for Oona? Arthur leaned over the iron railing. He wore his best leather jacket, his cleanest T-shirt, his darkest jeans. He had the stroller with him. Here to join the party?

The nanny smiled, so as not to discourage the bit of brightness he'd brought with him. Not today, Daddy, she said, still smiling. Please wait while I bring Oona to you.

The nanny closed and bolted the kitchen door. But before turning the lock she looked up at Arthur once more in a friendly way, a kind way that said I appreciate you've taken the time to come find your daughter. Because that's what any decent person does: they say hello to goodness, no matter how small, how tangled. Then someday the goodness will roar like a lion and shine like the sun. Just say hello. Hello! Hello! That's all there is to it, said the nanny to William and Oona.

In the foyer, she zipped Oona's jacket and smoothed the lumps of caught down. Tucked deep in a side pocket she found a hand-knit strawberry cap, maybe something from Oona's toddler life.

Who made this pretty thing? Tiny, perfect, the nanny folded it carefully and put it back where it belonged. Oona watched the cap come and go. She kept her head down low and didn't cry.

Say goodbye to your friend, now, William.

But William couldn't say goodbye after all that stuff about hello.

Come, William, said the nanny. A nod will do. No? All right then. How about we open up this door for your daddy? What do we say to that, Oona?

A question with an answer she knew by heart. Oona twisted the knob and there he was. Hi, Daddy! Hi! Right there. Hi! Right there. Right there.

For L.S.B. with love